D0116366

STONE ARCH BOOKS
a capstone imprint

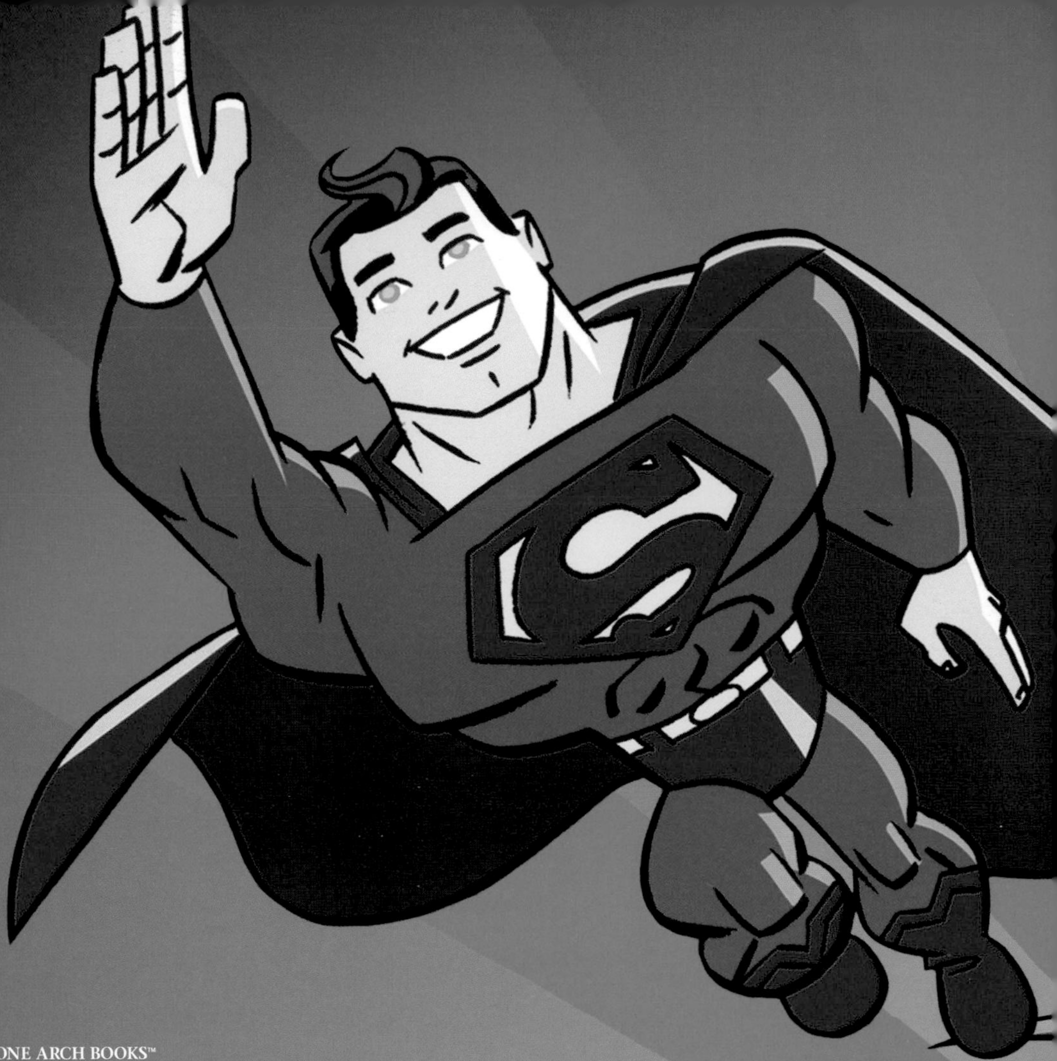

STONE ARCH BOOKS™
Published in 2013
A Capstone Imprint
1710 Roe Crest Drive
North Mankato, MN 56003
www.capstonepub.com

Originally published by DC Comics in
the U.S. in single magazine form as
DC Super Friends #8.

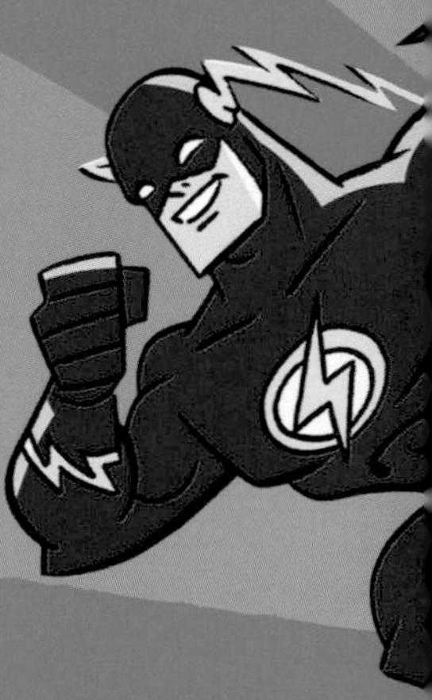

Cataloging-in-Publication Data is available at the
Library of Congress website:
ISBN: 978-1-4342-4703-2 (library binding)

Summary: It's Halloween, and the Scarecrow is on the
prowl! But nothing can scare the Super Friends!

STONE ARCH BOOKS
Ashley C. Andersen Zantop *Publisher*
Michael Dahl *Editorial Director*
Donald Lemke & Julie Gassman *Editors*
Heather Kindseth *Creative Director*
Brann Garvey *Designer*
Kathy McColley *Production Specialist*

DC COMICS
Rachel Gluckstern *Original U.S. Editor*

DC Comics
1700 Broadway, New York, NY 10019
A Warner Bros. Entertainment Company

Printed and bound in the USA.
009770R

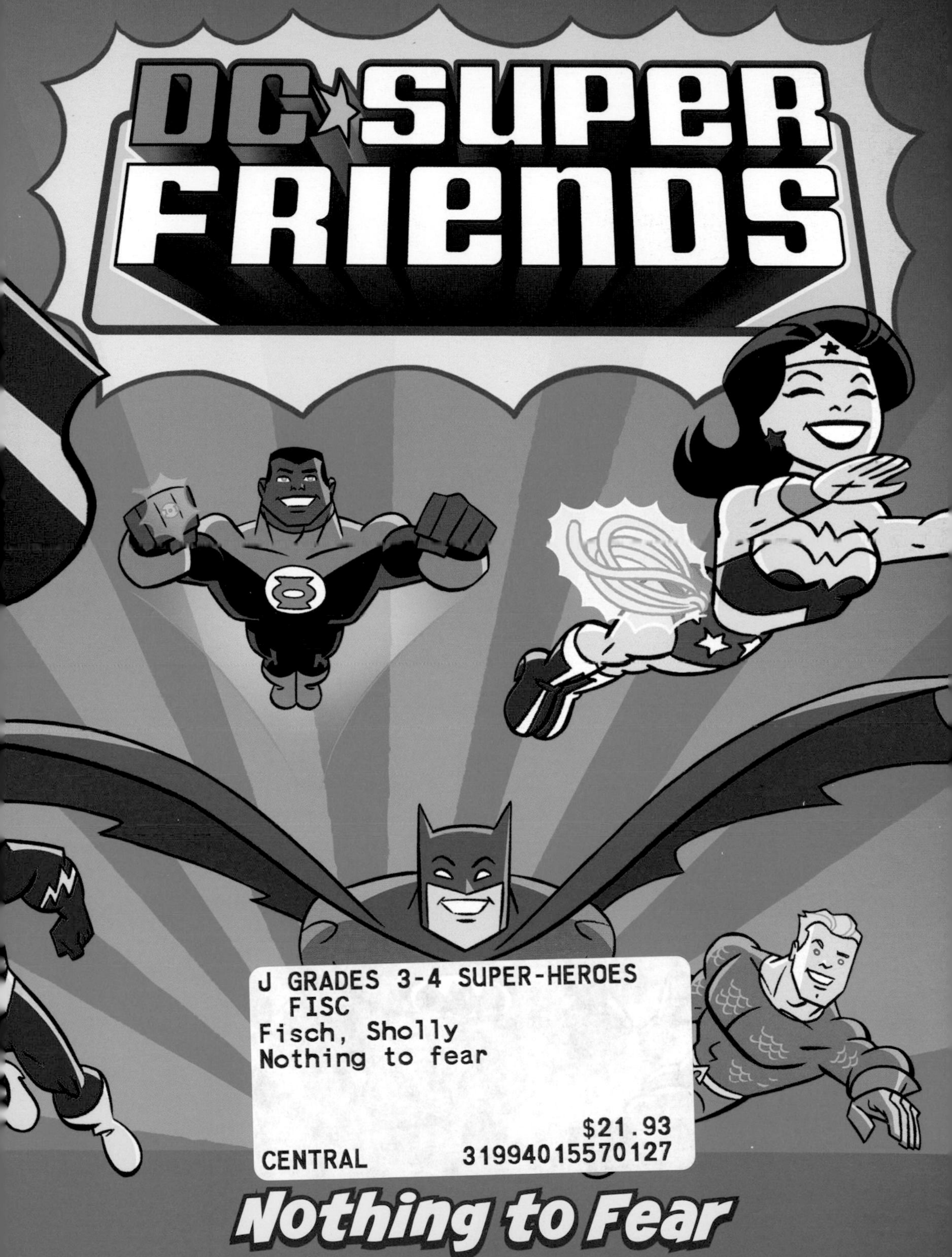
DC SUPER FRIENDS

Nothing to Fear

Sholly Fisch ....writer
Stewart McKenny ....penciler
Dan Davis ....inker
Heroic Age .... colorist
Randy Gentile ....letterer
J. Bone ....cover artist

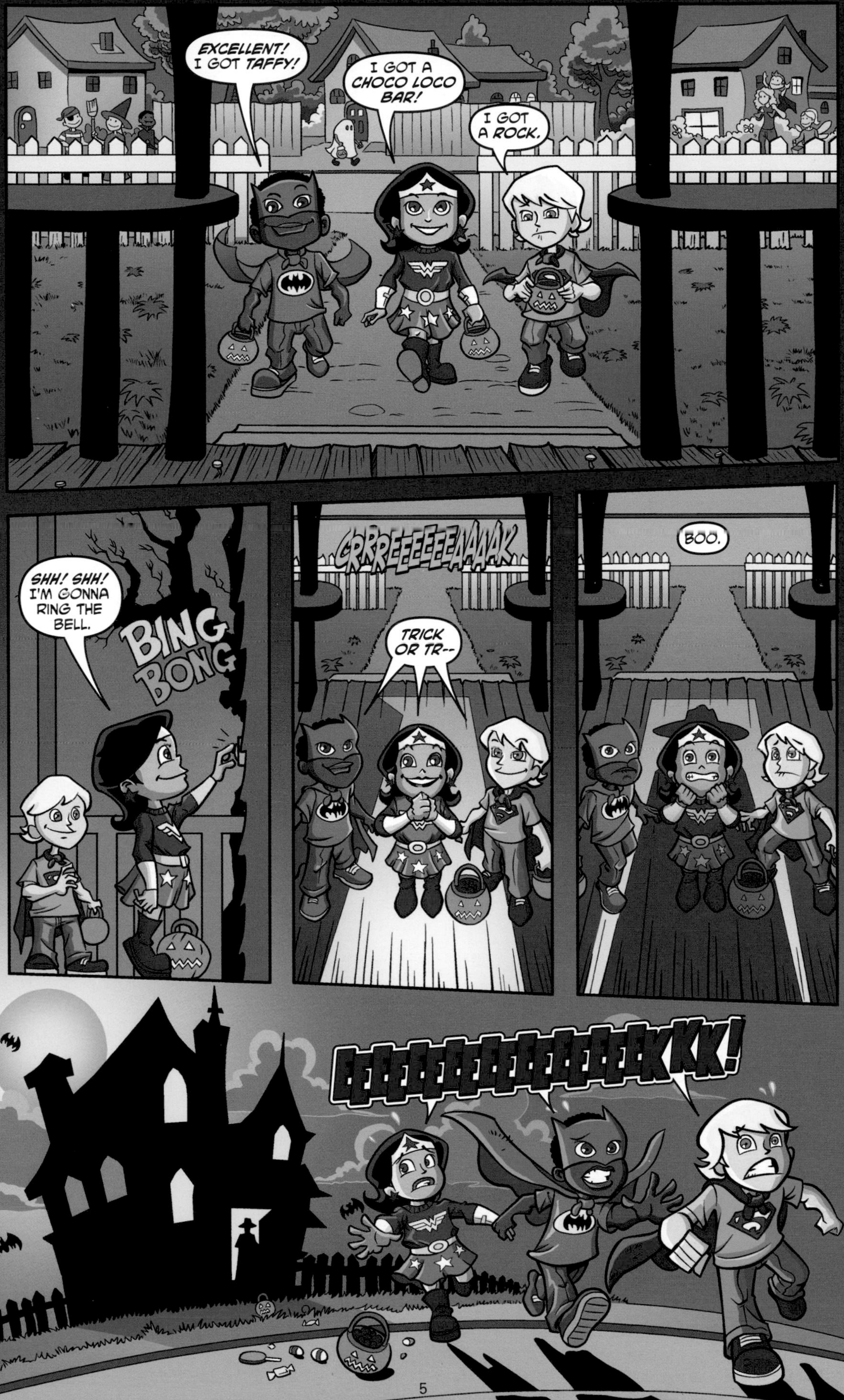

EXCELLENT! I GOT TAFFY!
I GOT A CHOCO LOCO BAR!
I GOT A ROCK.
SHH! SHH! I'M GONNA RING THE BELL.
BING BONG
CRRREEEEEEAAAAK
TRICK OR TR--
BOO.
EEEEEEEEEEEEEEEEKKK!

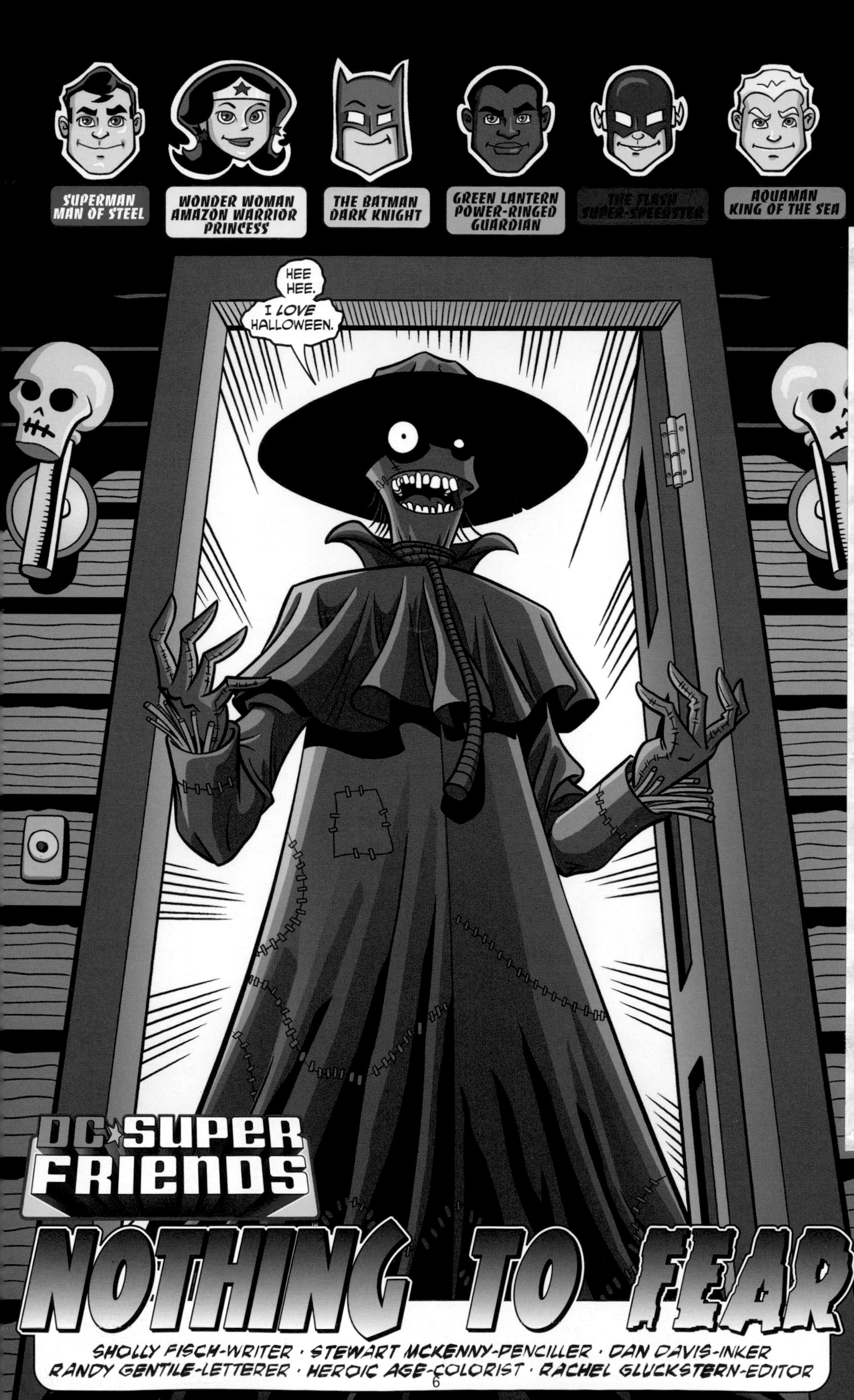
SUPERMAN MAN OF STEEL
WONDER WOMAN AMAZON WARRIOR PRINCESS
THE BATMAN DARK KNIGHT
GREEN LANTERN POWER-RINGED GUARDIAN
THE FLASH SUPER-SPEEDSTER
AQUAMAN KING OF THE SEA
HEE HEE. I LOVE HALLOWEEN.
DC SUPER FRIENDS
NOTHING TO FEAR
SHOLLY FISCH-WRITER · STEWART MCKENNY-PENCILLER · DAN DAVIS-INKER
RANDY GENTILE-LETTERER · HEROIC AGE-COLORIST · RACHEL GLUCKSTERN-EDITOR

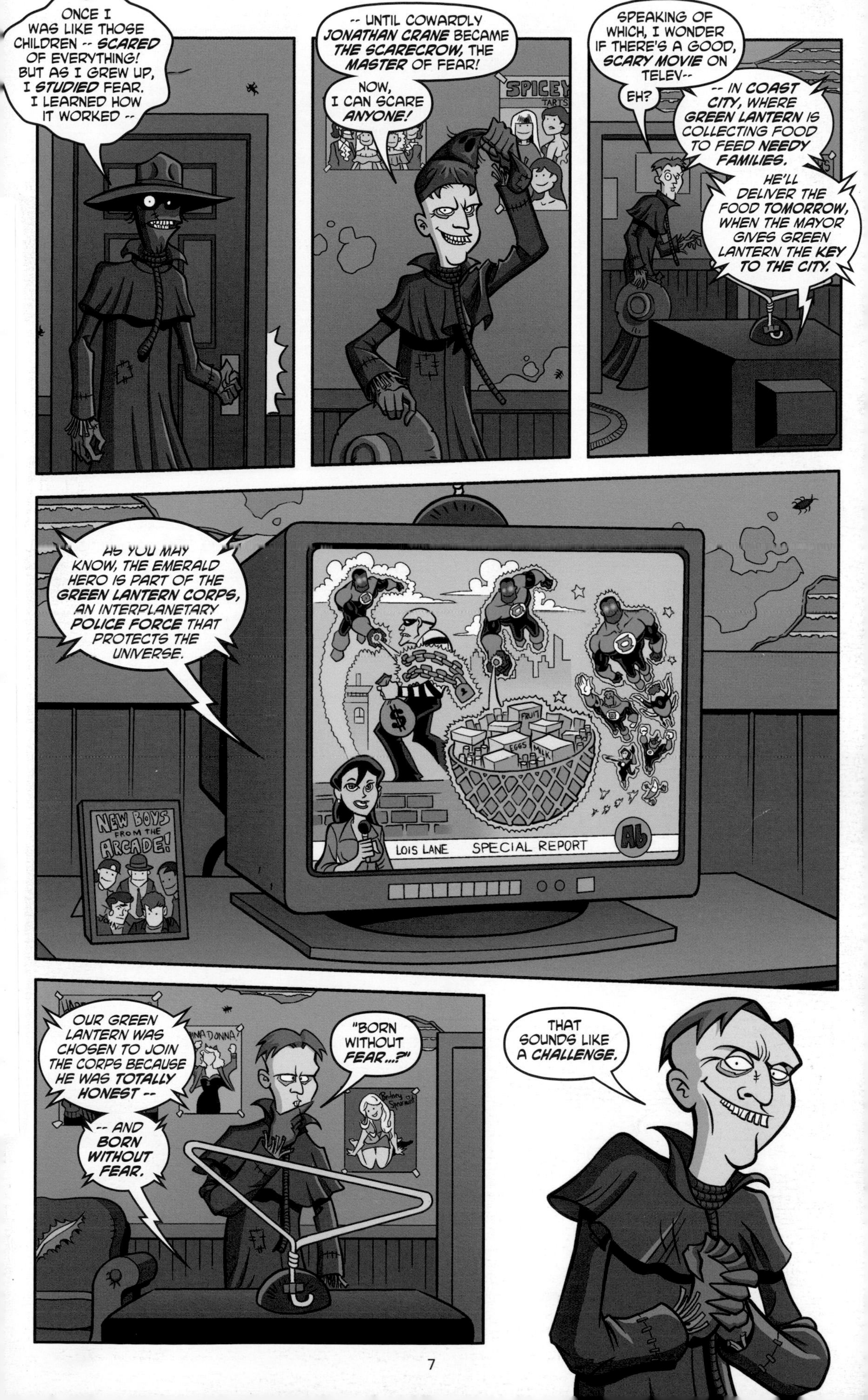
ONCE I WAS LIKE THOSE CHILDREN -- SCARED OF EVERYTHING! BUT AS I GREW UP, I STUDIED FEAR. I LEARNED HOW IT WORKED --
-- UNTIL COWARDLY JONATHAN CRANE BECAME THE SCARECROW, THE MASTER OF FEAR!
NOW, I CAN SCARE ANYONE!
SPICEY TARTS
SPEAKING OF WHICH, I WONDER IF THERE'S A GOOD, SCARY MOVIE ON TELEV--
EH?
-- IN COAST CITY, WHERE GREEN LANTERN IS COLLECTING FOOD TO FEED NEEDY FAMILIES.
HE'LL DELIVER THE FOOD TOMORROW, WHEN THE MAYOR GIVES GREEN LANTERN THE KEY TO THE CITY.
AS YOU MAY KNOW, THE EMERALD HERO IS PART OF THE GREEN LANTERN CORPS, AN INTERPLANETARY POLICE FORCE THAT PROTECTS THE UNIVERSE.
FRUIT
EGGS
MILK
LOIS LANE
SPECIAL REPORT
NEW BOYS FROM THE ARCADE!
OUR GREEN LANTERN WAS CHOSEN TO JOIN THE CORPS BECAUSE HE WAS TOTALLY HONEST --
-- AND BORN WITHOUT FEAR.
"BORN WITHOUT FEAR...?"
THAT SOUNDS LIKE A CHALLENGE.

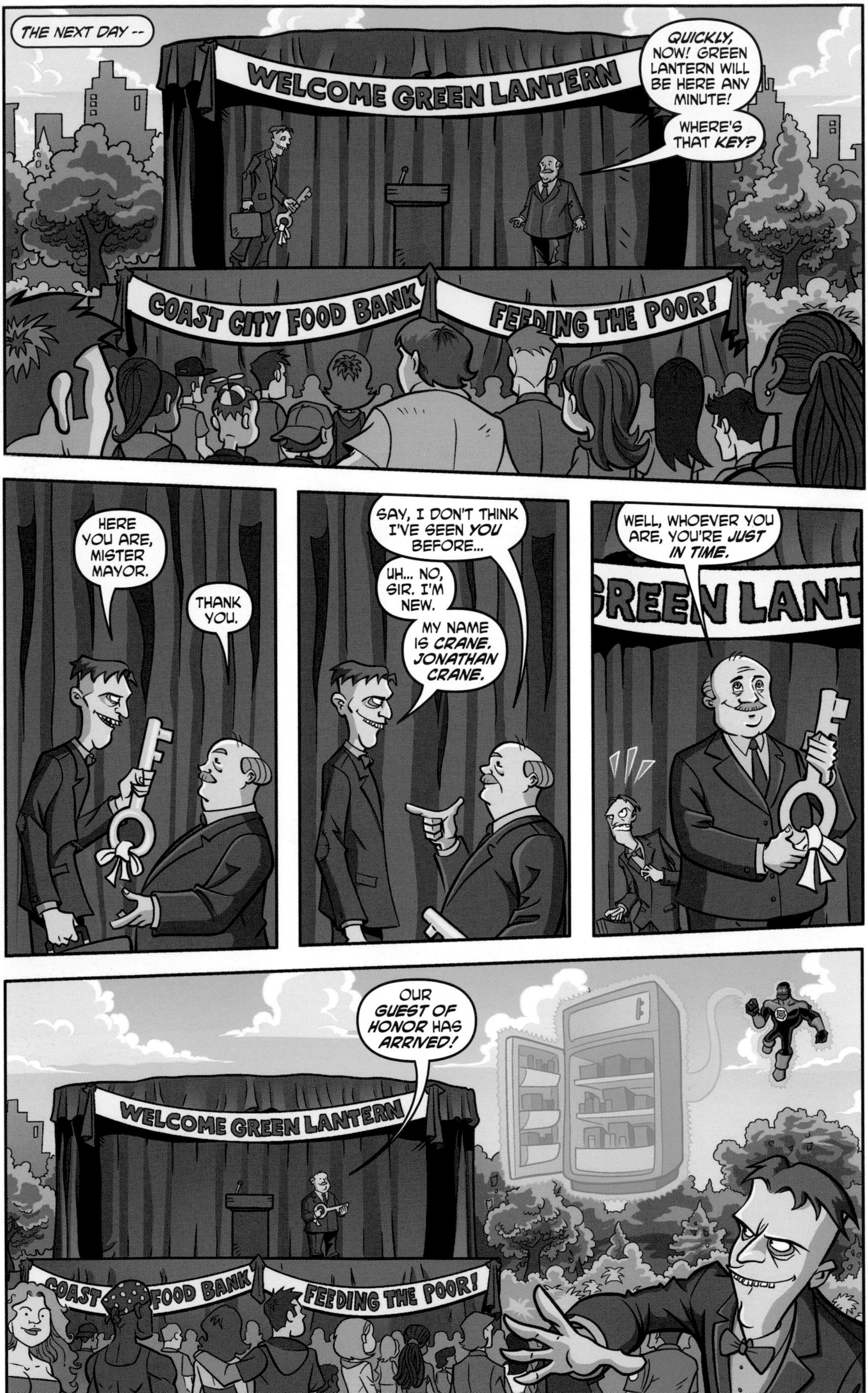
THE NEXT DAY --
WELCOME GREEN LANTERN
QUICKLY, NOW! GREEN LANTERN WILL BE HERE ANY MINUTE!
WHERE'S THAT KEY?
COAST CITY FOOD BANK
FEEDING THE POOR!
HERE YOU ARE, MISTER MAYOR.
THANK YOU.
SAY, I DON'T THINK I'VE SEEN YOU BEFORE...
UH... NO, SIR. I'M NEW.
MY NAME IS CRANE. JONATHAN CRANE.
WELL, WHOEVER YOU ARE, YOU'RE JUST IN TIME.
GREEN LANT
OUR GUEST OF HONOR HAS ARRIVED!
WELCOME GREEN LANTERN
COAST FOOD BANK
FEEDING THE POOR!

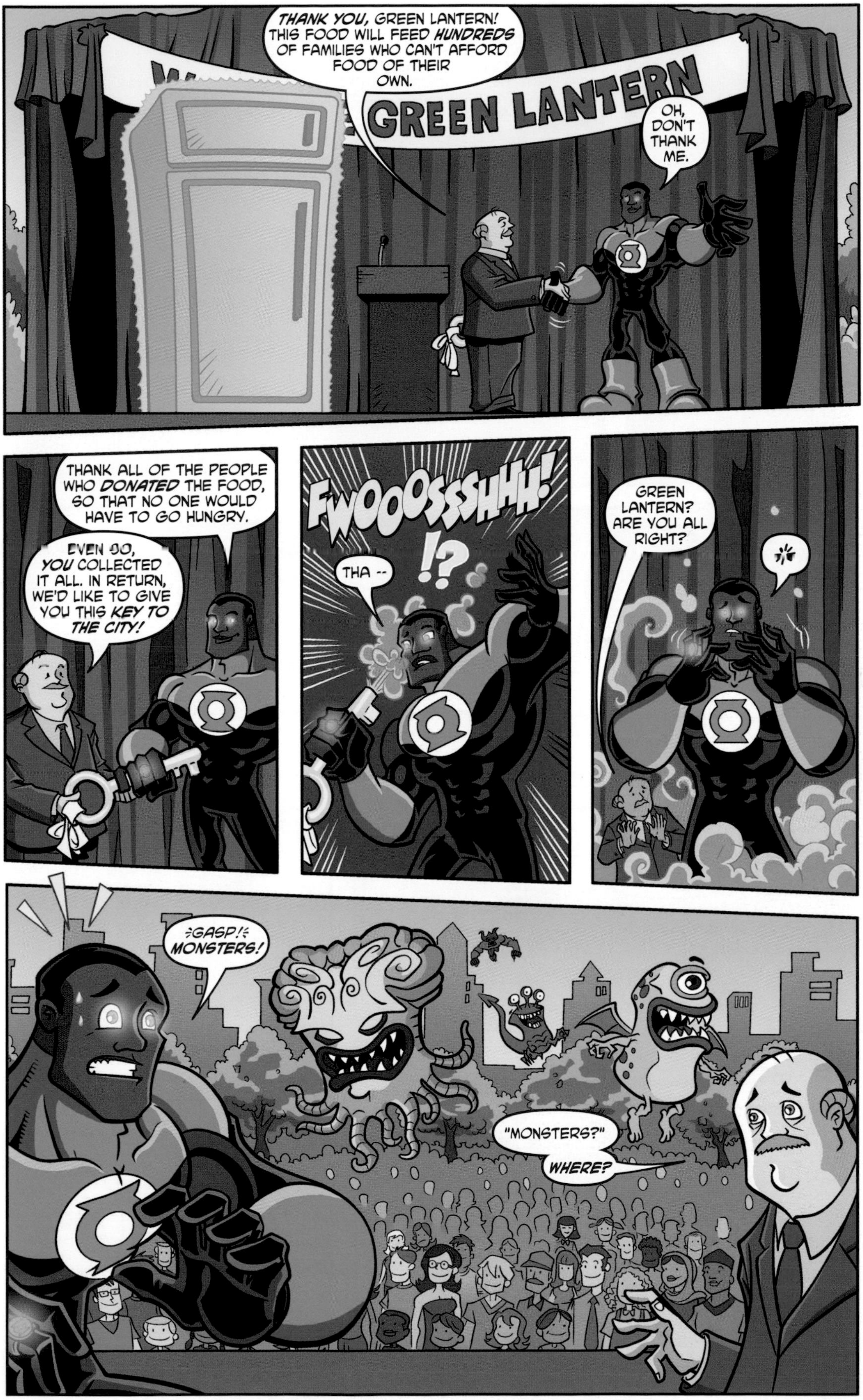
THANK YOU, GREEN LANTERN! THIS FOOD WILL FEED HUNDREDS OF FAMILIES WHO CAN'T AFFORD FOOD OF THEIR OWN.
GREEN LANTERN
OH, DON'T THANK ME.
THANK ALL OF THE PEOPLE WHO DONATED THE FOOD, SO THAT NO ONE WOULD HAVE TO GO HUNGRY.
EVEN SO, YOU COLLECTED IT ALL. IN RETURN, WE'D LIKE TO GIVE YOU THIS KEY TO THE CITY!
FWOOOSSSHHH!
THA --
!?
GREEN LANTERN? ARE YOU ALL RIGHT?
GASP! MONSTERS!
"MONSTERS?"
WHERE?

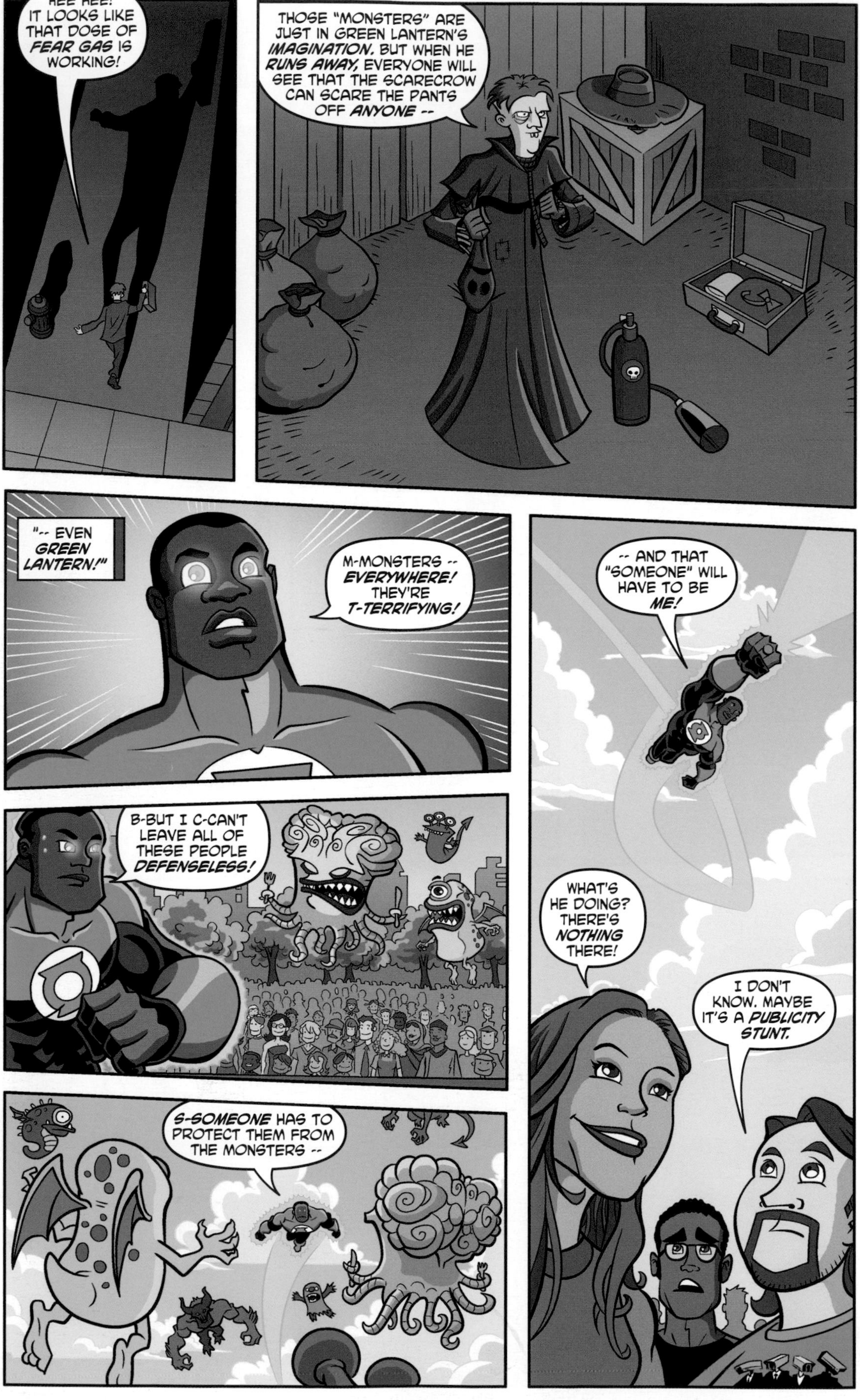
HEE HEE! IT LOOKS LIKE THAT DOSE OF FEAR GAS IS WORKING!
THOSE "MONSTERS" ARE JUST IN GREEN LANTERN'S IMAGINATION. BUT WHEN HE RUNS AWAY, EVERYONE WILL SEE THAT THE SCARECROW CAN SCARE THE PANTS OFF ANYONE --
"-- EVEN GREEN LANTERN!"
M-MONSTERS -- EVERYWHERE! THEY'RE T-TERRIFYING!
B-BUT I C-CAN'T LEAVE ALL OF THESE PEOPLE DEFENSELESS!
S-SOMEONE HAS TO PROTECT THEM FROM THE MONSTERS --
-- AND THAT "SOMEONE" WILL HAVE TO BE ME!
WHAT'S HE DOING? THERE'S NOTHING THERE!
I DON'T KNOW. MAYBE IT'S A PUBLICITY STUNT.

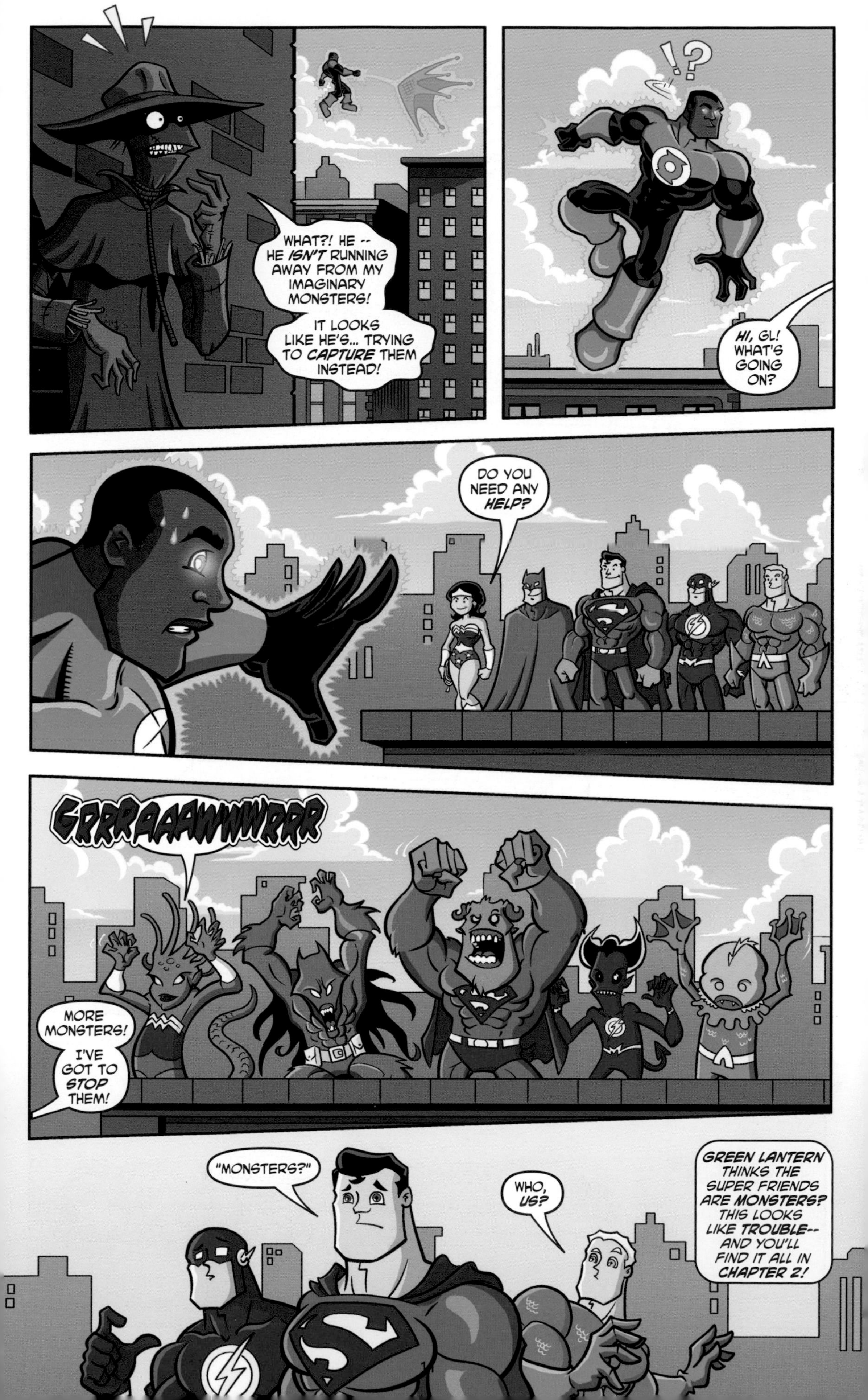

WHAT?! HE -- HE *ISN'T* RUNNING AWAY FROM MY IMAGINARY MONSTERS!
IT LOOKS LIKE HE'S... TRYING TO *CAPTURE* THEM INSTEAD!
!?
HI, GL! WHAT'S GOING ON?
DO YOU NEED ANY *HELP?*
GRRRAAAWWWRRR
MORE MONSTERS!
I'VE GOT TO *STOP* THEM!
"MONSTERS?"
WHO, *US?*
GREEN LANTERN THINKS THE SUPER FRIENDS *ARE MONSTERS?* THIS LOOKS LIKE *TROUBLE--* AND YOU'LL FIND IT ALL IN *CHAPTER 2!*

NOTHING TO FEAR -- CHAPTER 2

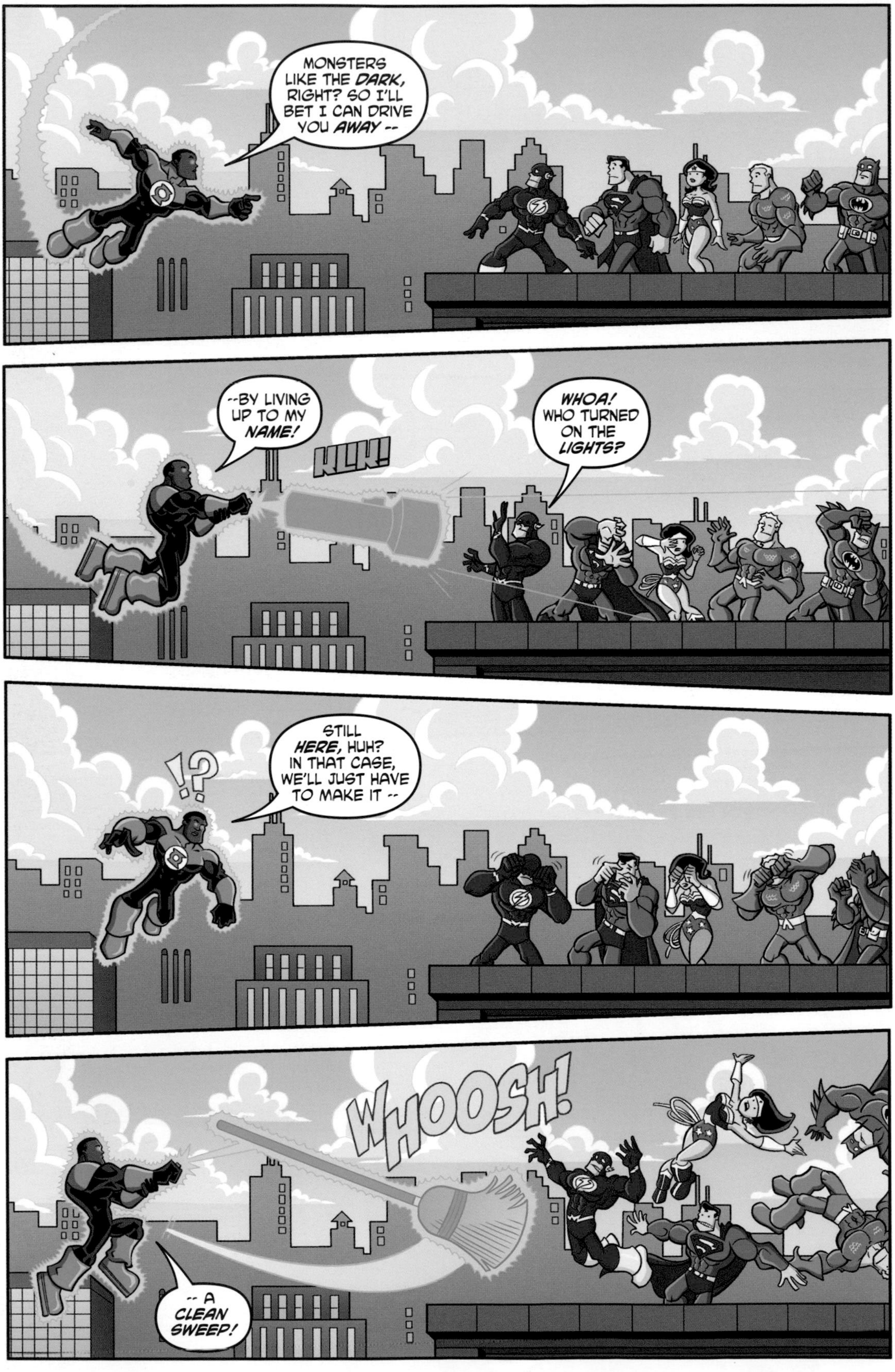
MONSTERS LIKE THE DARK, RIGHT? SO I'LL BET I CAN DRIVE YOU AWAY --
--BY LIVING UP TO MY NAME!
KLIK!
WHOA! WHO TURNED ON THE LIGHTS?
!?
STILL HERE, HUH? IN THAT CASE, WE'LL JUST HAVE TO MAKE IT --
WHOOSH!
-- A CLEAN SWEEP!

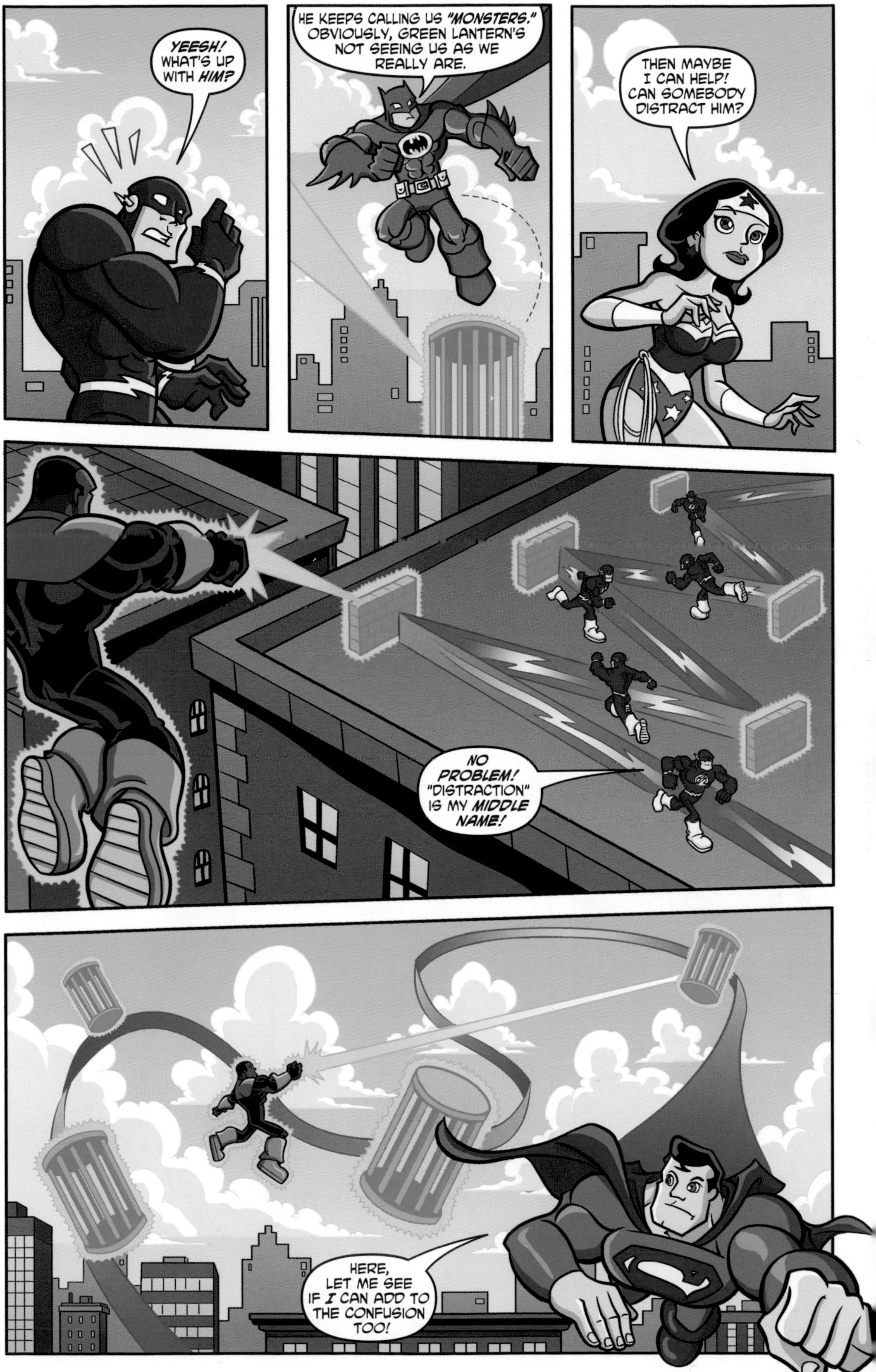
YEESH! WHAT'S UP WITH HIM?
HE KEEPS CALLING US "MONSTERS." OBVIOUSLY, GREEN LANTERN'S NOT SEEING US AS WE REALLY ARE.
THEN MAYBE I CAN HELP! CAN SOMEBODY DISTRACT HIM?
NO PROBLEM! "DISTRACTION" IS MY MIDDLE NAME!
HERE, LET ME SEE IF I CAN ADD TO THE CONFUSION TOO!

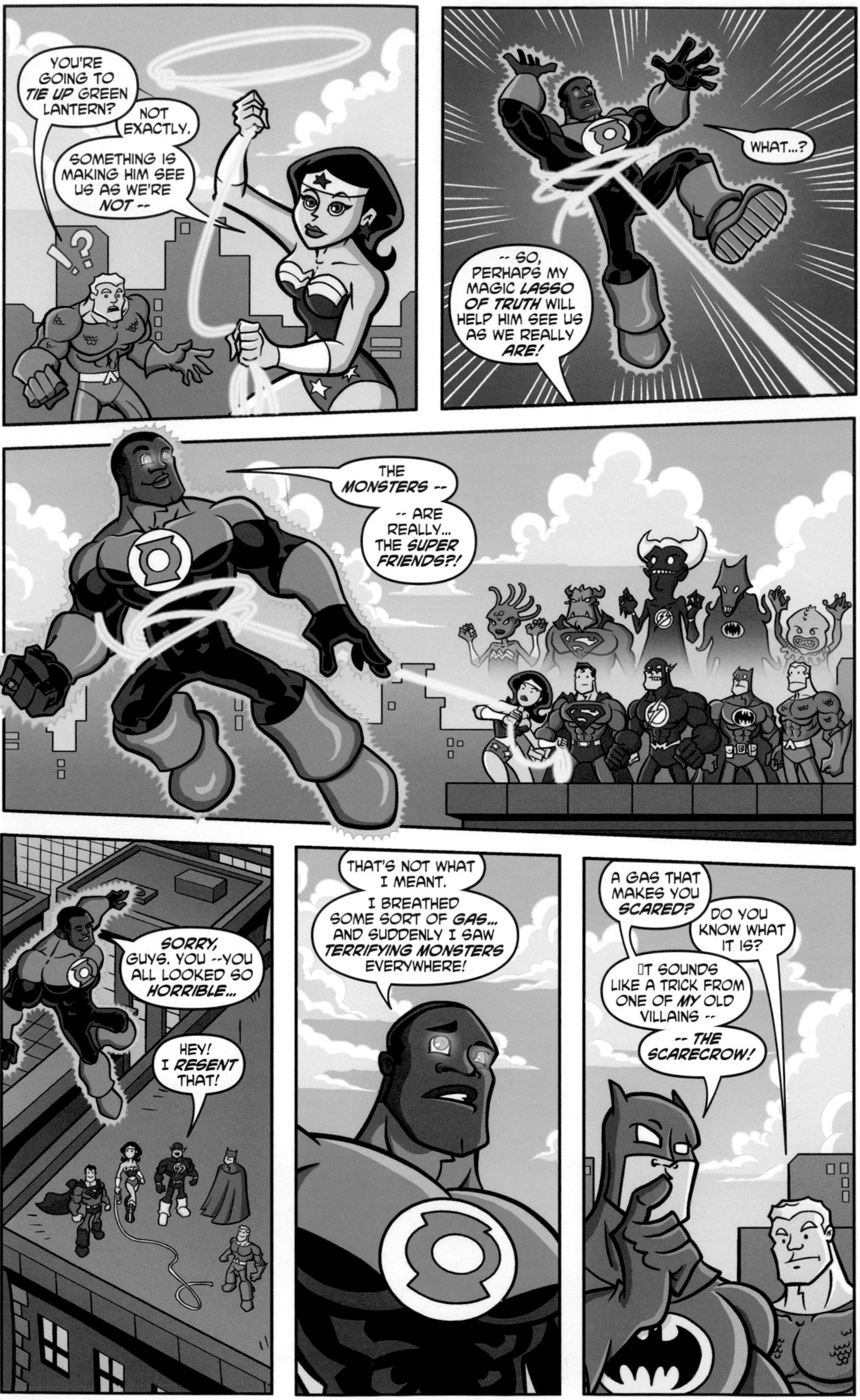

YOU'RE GOING TO *TIE UP* GREEN LANTERN?
NOT EXACTLY.
SOMETHING IS MAKING HIM SEE US AS WE'RE *NOT* --
!?
WHAT...?
-- SO, PERHAPS MY MAGIC *LASSO OF TRUTH* WILL HELP HIM SEE US AS WE REALLY *ARE!*
THE *MONSTERS* --
-- ARE REALLY... THE *SUPER FRIENDS?!*
SORRY, GUYS. YOU --YOU ALL LOOKED SO *HORRIBLE...*
HEY! I *RESENT* THAT!
THAT'S NOT WHAT I MEANT.
I BREATHED SOME SORT OF *GAS...* AND SUDDENLY I SAW *TERRIFYING MONSTERS* EVERYWHERE!
A GAS THAT MAKES YOU *SCARED?*
DO YOU KNOW WHAT IT IS?
IT SOUNDS LIKE A TRICK FROM ONE OF *MY* OLD VILLAINS --
-- *THE SCARECROW!*

THE SCARECROW?

WHY WOULD ONE OF *YOUR* VILLAINS GO AFTER *ME*?

I DON'T KNOW... BUT WE CAN *ASK* HIM! ACCORDING TO MY *SUPER-VISION*, THE SCARECROW IS --

-- *RIGHT OVER THERE!*

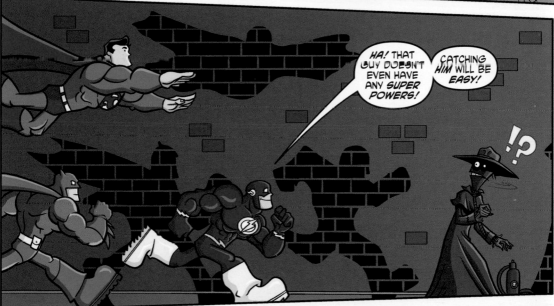

HA! THAT GUY DOESN'T EVEN HAVE ANY *SUPER POWERS!*

CATCHING *HIM* WILL BE *EASY!*

!?

THINK AGAIN! YOU WON'T EVEN BE ABLE TO *USE* YOUR OWN POWERS!

BECAUSE *I* COMMAND THE GREATEST POWER OF ALL --

-- THE POWER OF *FEAR!*

WATCH OUT! IT'S MORE OF HIS *FEAR GAS!*

SSSSSSSSSSSS

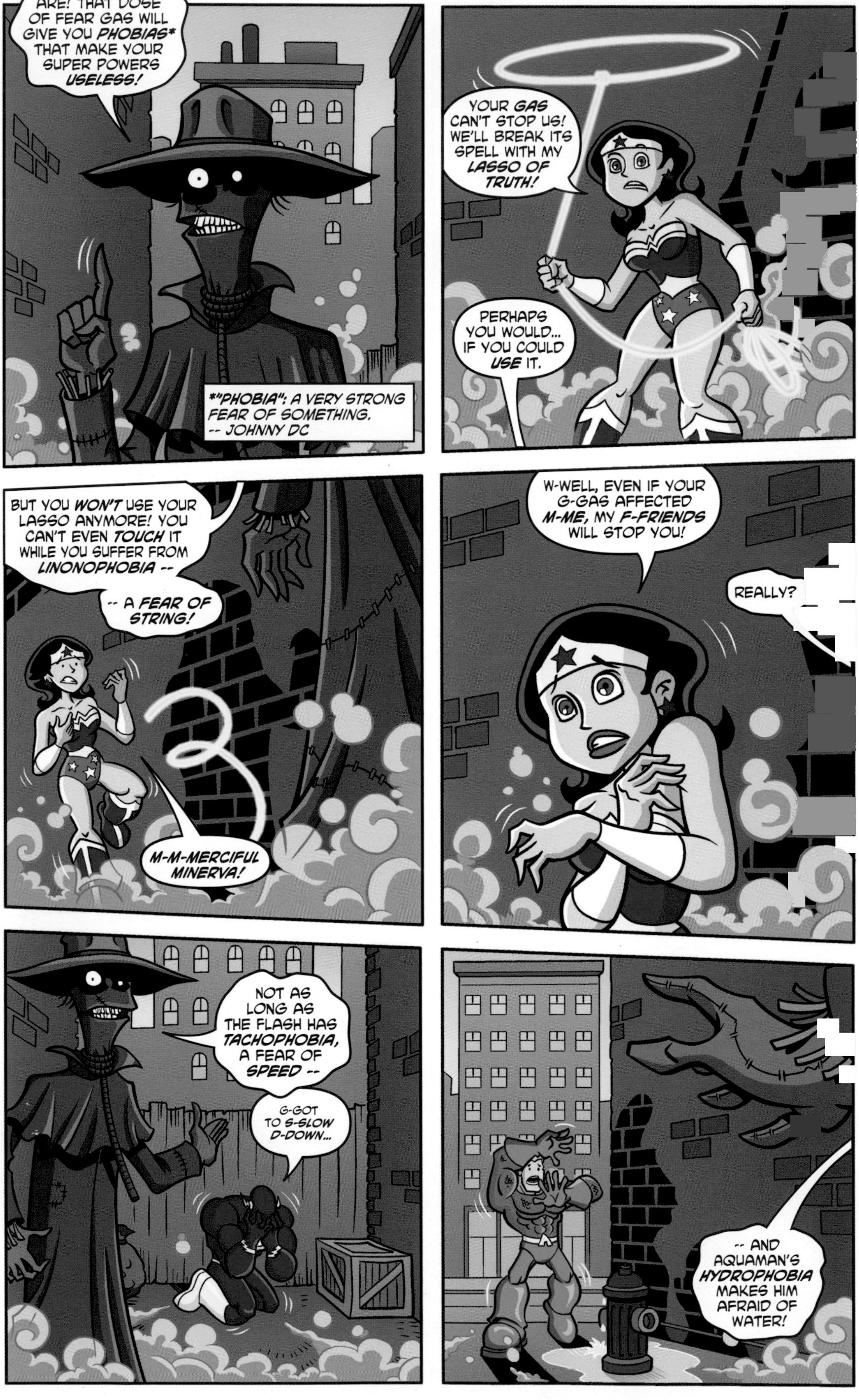
RIGHT YOU ARE! THAT DOSE OF FEAR GAS WILL GIVE YOU PHOBIAS* THAT MAKE YOUR SUPER POWERS USELESS!
*"PHOBIA": A VERY STRONG FEAR OF SOMETHING. -- JOHNNY DC
YOUR GAS CAN'T STOP US! WE'LL BREAK ITS SPELL WITH MY LASSO OF TRUTH!
PERHAPS YOU WOULD... IF YOU COULD USE IT.
BUT YOU WON'T USE YOUR LASSO ANYMORE! YOU CAN'T EVEN TOUCH IT WHILE YOU SUFFER FROM LINONOPHOBIA --
-- A FEAR OF STRING!
M-M-MERCIFUL MINERVA!
W-WELL, EVEN IF YOUR G-GAS AFFECTED M-ME, MY F-FRIENDS WILL STOP YOU!
REALLY?
NOT AS LONG AS THE FLASH HAS TACHOPHOBIA, A FEAR OF SPEED --
G-GOT TO S-SLOW D-DOWN...
-- AND AQUAMAN'S HYDROPHOBIA MAKES HIM AFRAID OF WATER!

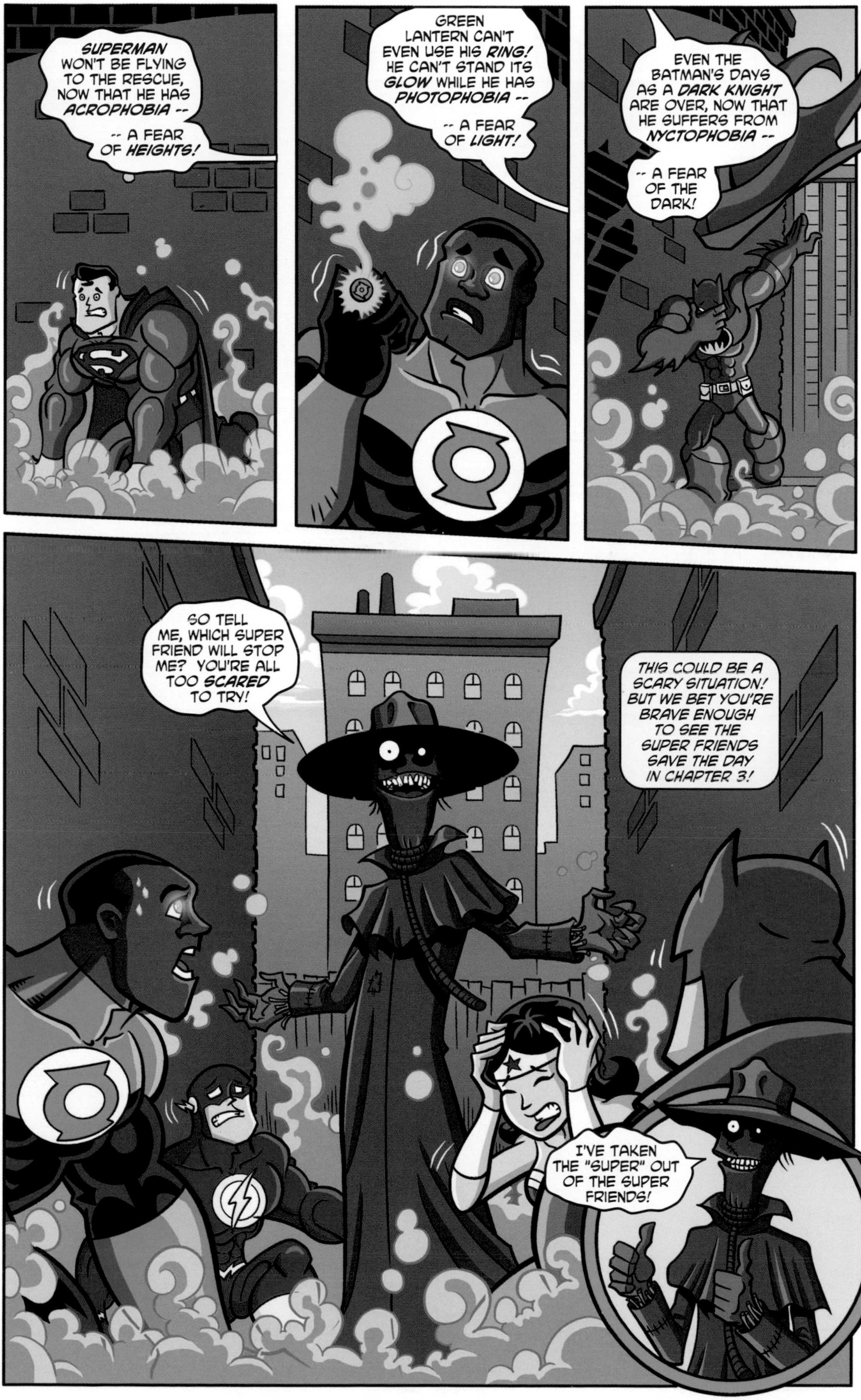
SUPERMAN WON'T BE FLYING TO THE RESCUE, NOW THAT HE HAS ACROPHOBIA --
-- A FEAR OF HEIGHTS!
GREEN LANTERN CAN'T EVEN USE HIS RING! HE CAN'T STAND ITS GLOW WHILE HE HAS PHOTOPHOBIA --
-- A FEAR OF LIGHT!
EVEN THE BATMAN'S DAYS AS A DARK KNIGHT ARE OVER, NOW THAT HE SUFFERS FROM NYCTOPHOBIA --
-- A FEAR OF THE DARK!
SO TELL ME, WHICH SUPER FRIEND WILL STOP ME? YOU'RE ALL TOO SCARED TO TRY!
THIS COULD BE A SCARY SITUATION! BUT WE BET YOU'RE BRAVE ENOUGH TO SEE THE SUPER FRIENDS SAVE THE DAY IN CHAPTER 3!
I'VE TAKEN THE "SUPER" OUT OF THE SUPER FRIENDS!

NOTHING TO FEAR -- CHAPTER 3

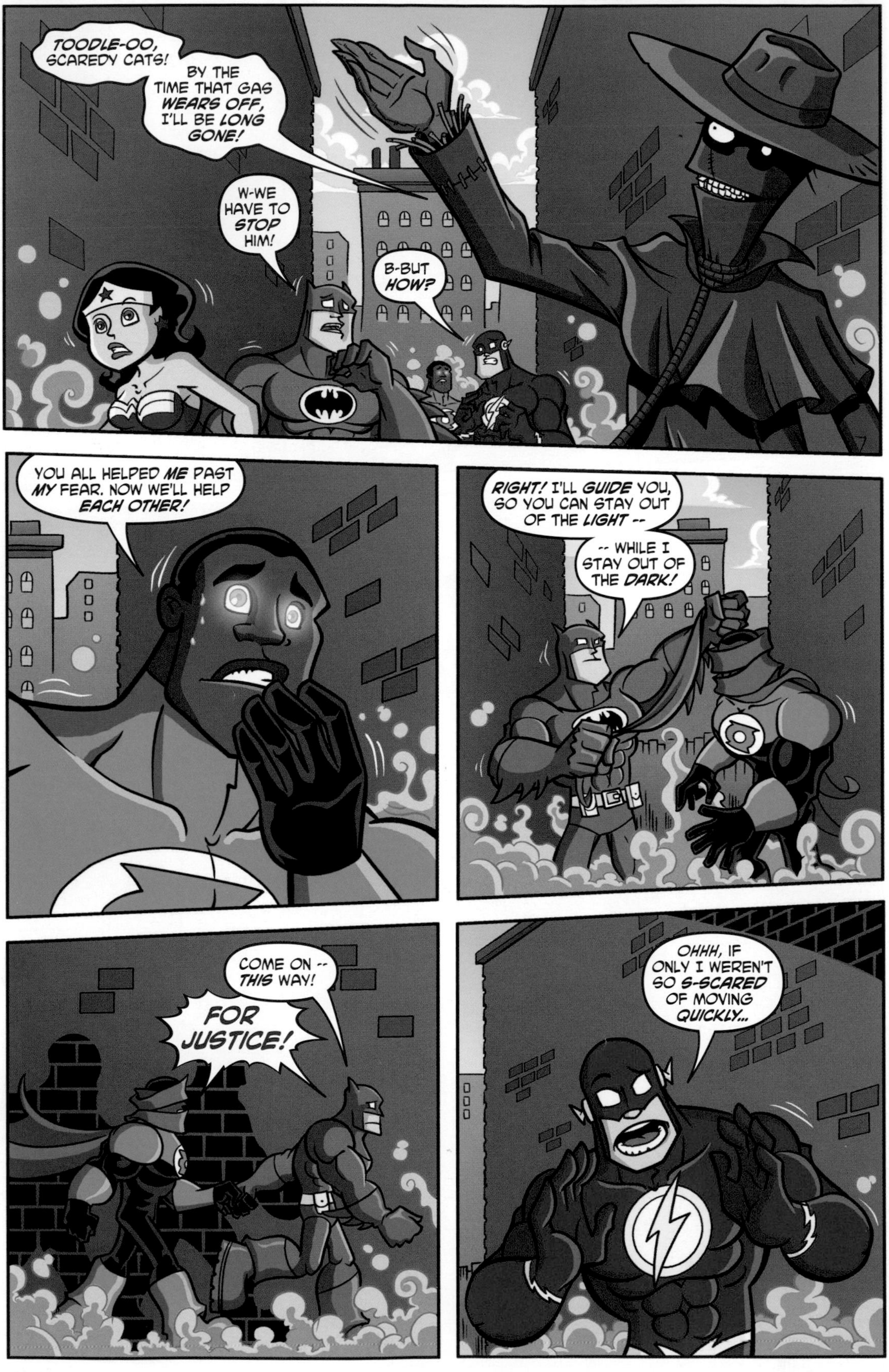
TOODLE-OO, SCAREDY CATS!
BY THE TIME THAT GAS WEARS OFF, I'LL BE LONG GONE!
W-WE HAVE TO STOP HIM!
B-BUT HOW?
YOU ALL HELPED ME PAST MY FEAR. NOW WE'LL HELP EACH OTHER!
RIGHT! I'LL GUIDE YOU, SO YOU CAN STAY OUT OF THE LIGHT --
-- WHILE I STAY OUT OF THE DARK!
COME ON -- THIS WAY!
FOR JUSTICE!
OHHH, IF ONLY I WEREN'T SO S-SCARED OF MOVING QUICKLY...

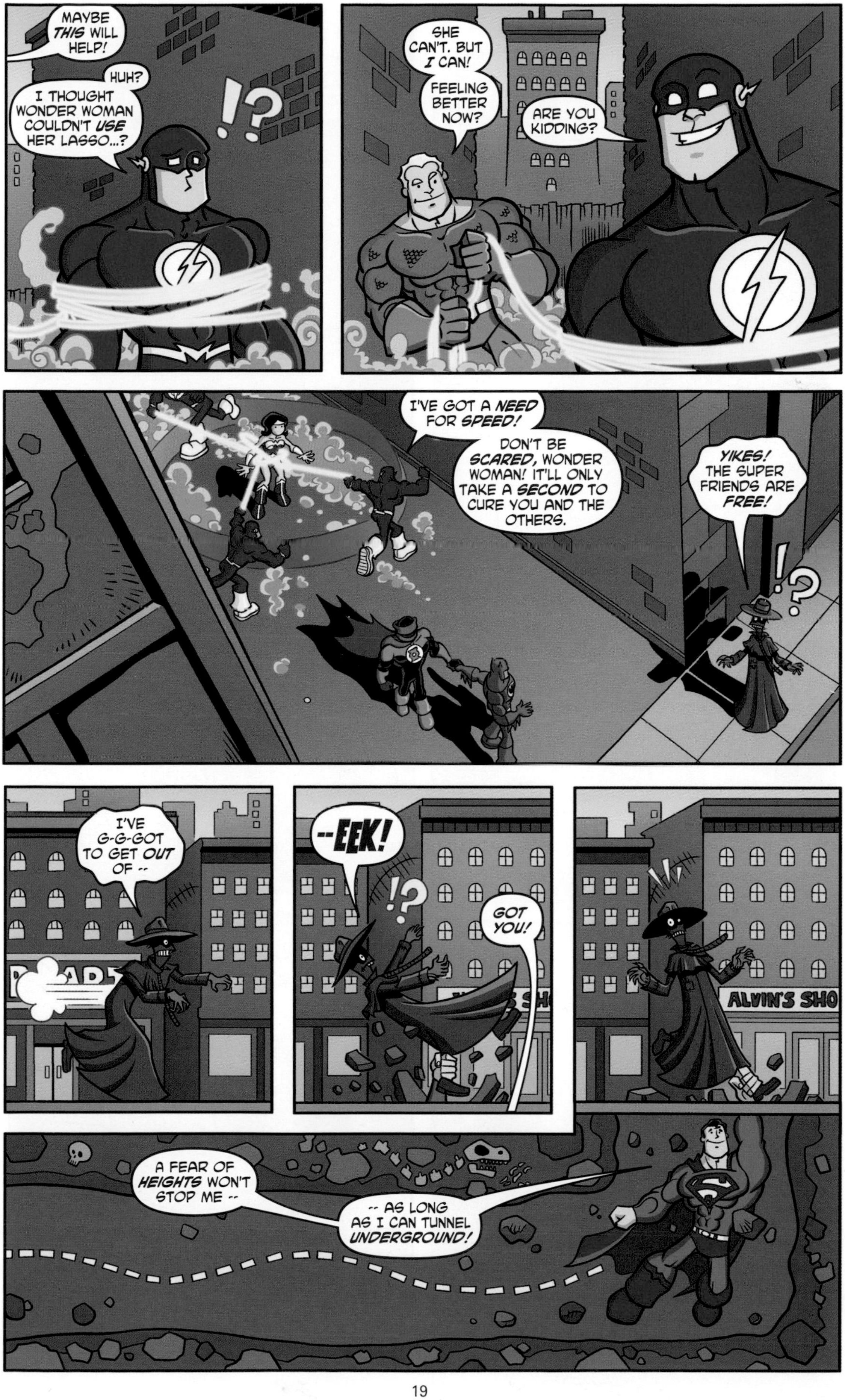
MAYBE THIS WILL HELP!
HUH?
I THOUGHT WONDER WOMAN COULDN'T USE HER LASSO...?
!?
SHE CAN'T. BUT I CAN!
FEELING BETTER NOW?
ARE YOU KIDDING?
I'VE GOT A NEED FOR SPEED!
DON'T BE SCARED, WONDER WOMAN! IT'LL ONLY TAKE A SECOND TO CURE YOU AND THE OTHERS.
YIKES! THE SUPER FRIENDS ARE FREE!
!?
I'VE G-G-GOT TO GET OUT OF --
--EEK!
!?
GOT YOU!
ALVIN'S SHO
A FEAR OF HEIGHTS WON'T STOP ME --
-- AS LONG AS I CAN TUNNEL UNDERGROUND!

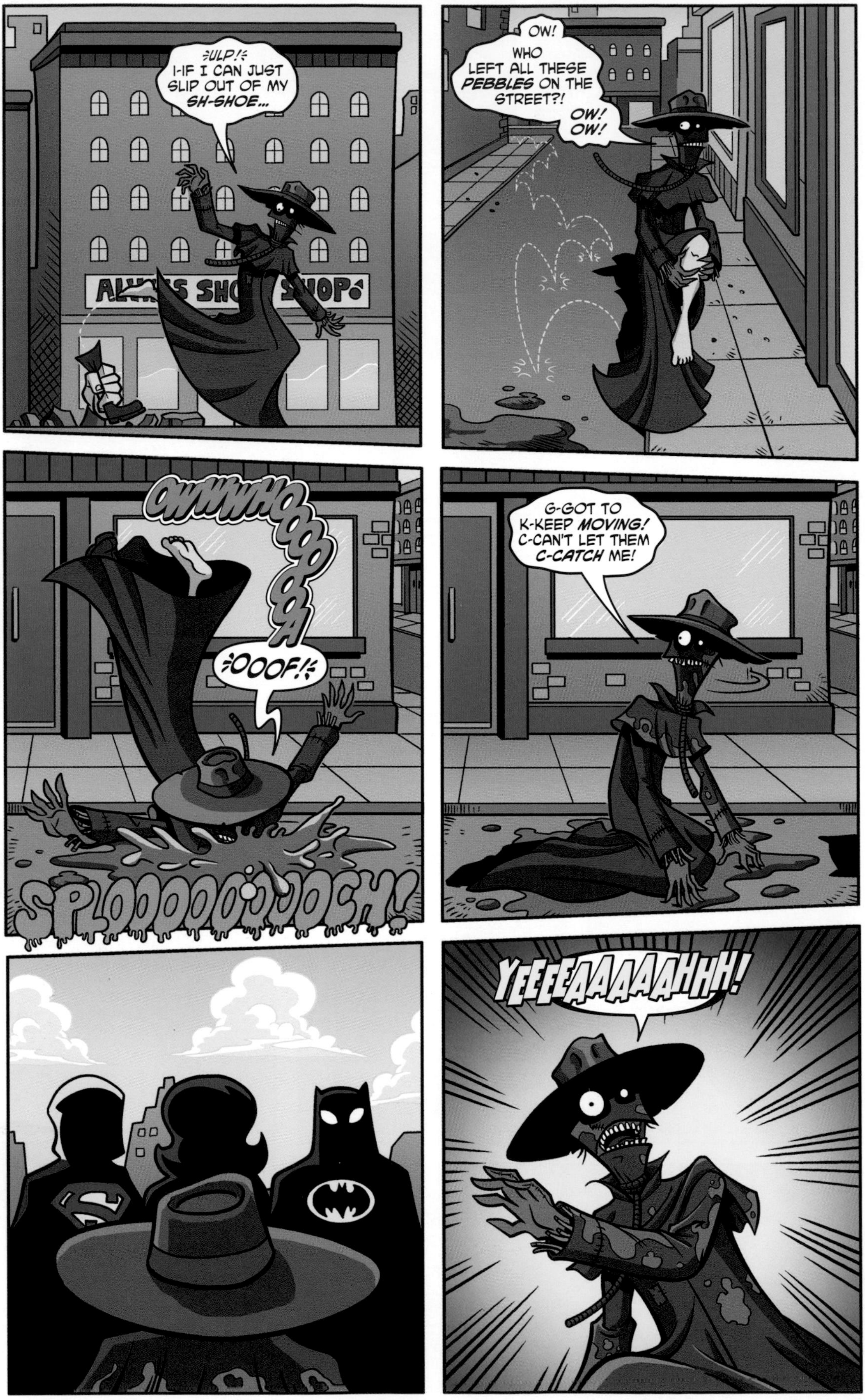
ULP!
I-IF I CAN JUST SLIP OUT OF MY SH-SHOE...
OW!
WHO LEFT ALL THESE PEBBLES ON THE STREET?!
OW! OW!
OWWWHOOOOOOOA
OOOF!
SPLOOOOOOOOCH!
G-GOT TO K-KEEP MOVING! C-CAN'T LET THEM C-CATCH ME!
YEEEEAAAAAAHHH!

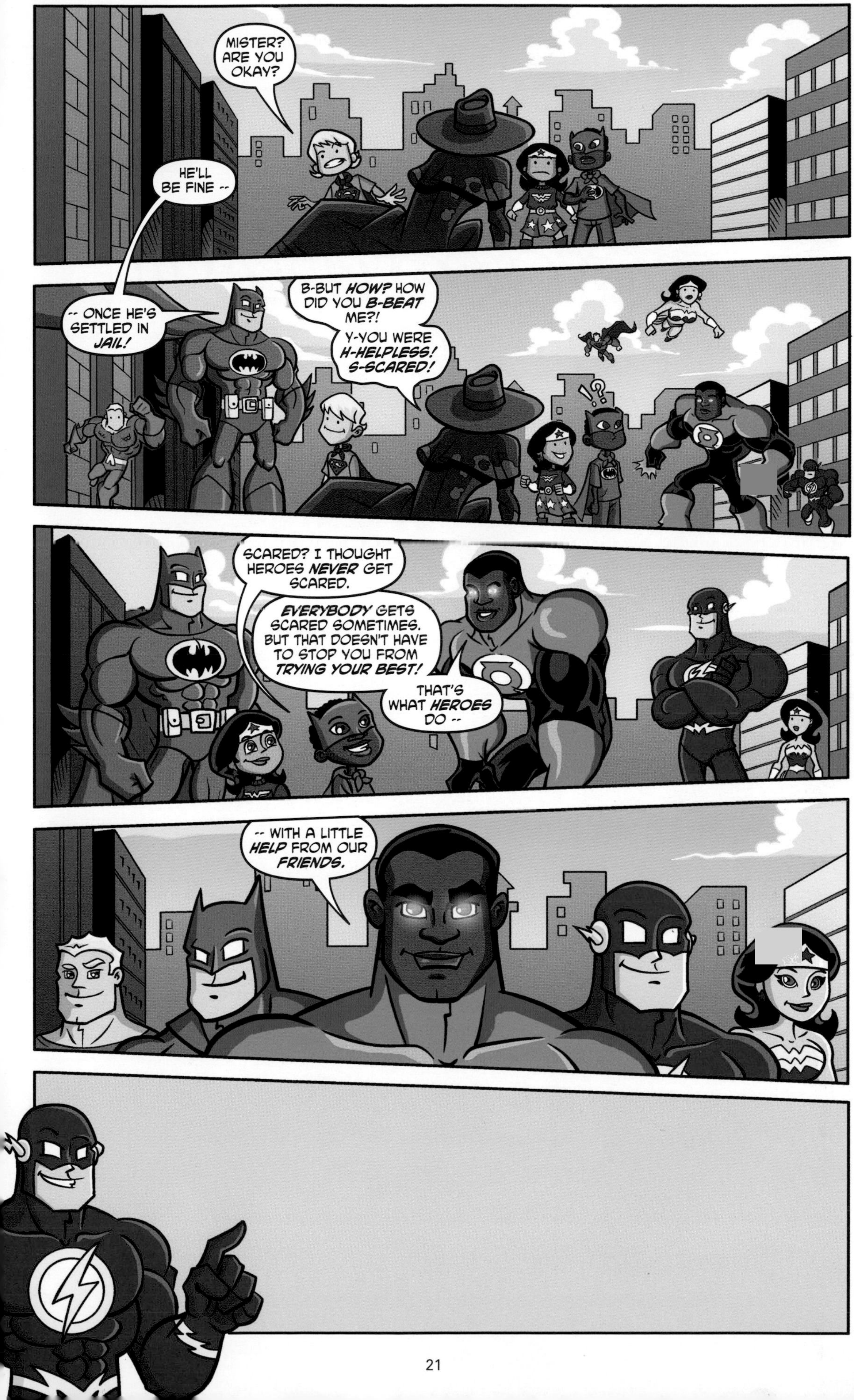
MISTER? ARE YOU OKAY?
HE'LL BE FINE --
-- ONCE HE'S SETTLED IN JAIL!
B-BUT HOW? HOW DID YOU B-BEAT ME?!
Y-YOU WERE H-HELPLESS! S-SCARED!
!?
SCARED? I THOUGHT HEROES NEVER GET SCARED.
EVERYBODY GETS SCARED SOMETIMES. BUT THAT DOESN'T HAVE TO STOP YOU FROM TRYING YOUR BEST!
THAT'S WHAT HEROES DO --
-- WITH A LITTLE HELP FROM OUR FRIENDS.

ATTENTION, ALL SUPER FRIENDS!

HERE'S THIS BOOK'S SECRET MESSAGE:

PEVOY CYSOXRP ZBBU BEI CBY BINOYP

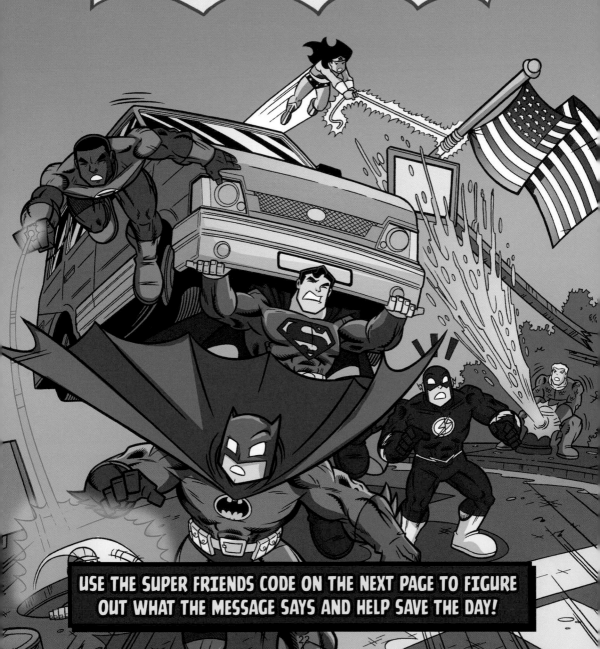

USE THE SUPER FRIENDS CODE ON THE NEXT PAGE TO FIGURE OUT WHAT THE MESSAGE SAYS AND HELP SAVE THE DAY!

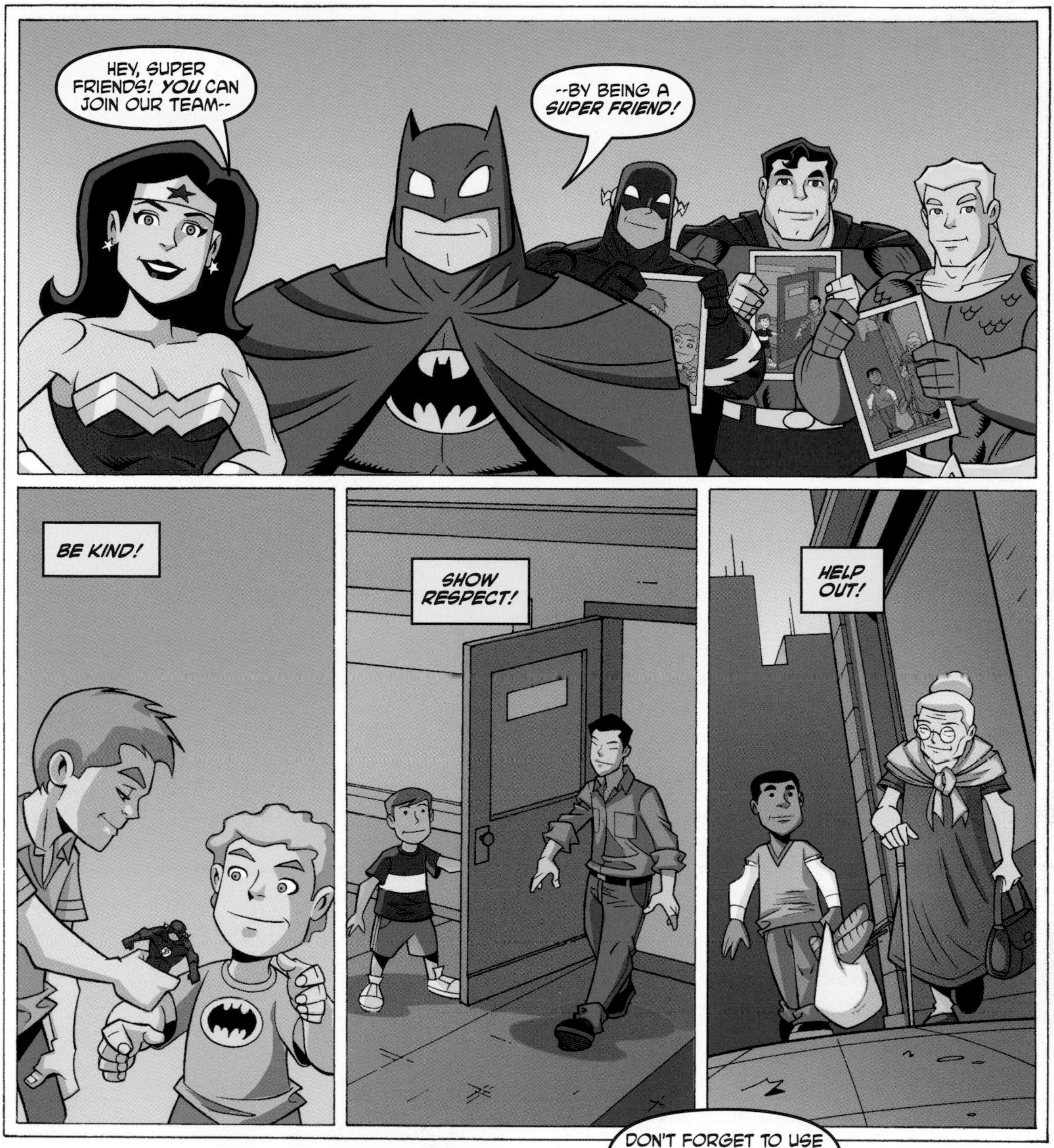
HEY, SUPER FRIENDS! YOU CAN JOIN OUR TEAM--
--BY BEING A SUPER FRIEND!
BE KIND!
SHOW RESPECT!
HELP OUT!

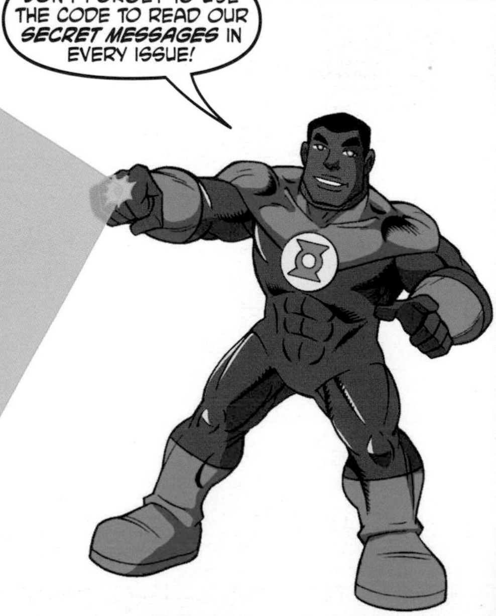
DON'T FORGET TO USE THE CODE TO READ OUR SECRET MESSAGES IN EVERY ISSUE!

SUPER FRIENDS SECRET CODE
(KEEP THIS AWAY FROM SUPER-VILLAINS!)

A = Q	J = Z	S = I
B = O	K = A	T = V
C = F	L = X	U = K
D = M	M = C	V = P
E = U	N = H	W = Y
F = J	O = E	X = N
G = W	P = S	Y = R
H = B	Q = G	Z = L
I = T	R = D	

KNOW YOUR SUPER FRIENDS!

SUPERMAN

Real Name: Clark Kent

Powers: Super-strength, super-speed, flight, super-senses, heat vision, invulnerability, super-breath

Origin: Just before the planet Krypton exploded, baby Kal-El escaped in a rocket to Earth. On Earth, he was adopted by a kind couple named Jonathan and Martha Kent.

BATMAN

Secret Identity: Bruce Wayne

Abilities: World's greatest detective, acrobat, escape artist

Origin: Orphaned at a young age, young millionaire Bruce Wayne promised to keep all people safe from crime. After training for many years, he put on costume that would scare criminals - the costume of Batman.

WONDER WOMAN

Secret Identity: Princess Diana

Powers: Super-strong, faster than normal humans, uses her bracelets as shields and magic lasso to make people tell the truth

Origin: Diana is the Princess of Paradise Island, the hidden home of the Amazons. When Diana was a baby, the Greek gods gave her special powers.

GREEN LANTERN

Secret Identity: John Stewart

Powers: Through the strength of willpower, Green Lantern's power ring can create anything he imagines

Origin: Led by the Guardians of the Universe, the Green Lantern Corps is an outer-space police force that keeps the whole universe safe. The Guardians chose John to protect Earth as our planet's Green Lantern.

THE FLASH

Secret Identity: Wally West

Powers: Flash uses his super-speed in many ways: he can run across water or up the side of a building, spin around to make a tornado, or vibrate his body to walk right through a wall

Origin: As a boy, Wally West became the super-fast Kid Flash when lightning hit a rack of chemicals that spilled on him. Today, he helps others as the Flash.

AQUAMAN

Real Name: King Orin or Arthur Curry

Powers: Breathes underwater, communicates with fish, swims at high speed, stronger than normal humans

Origin: Orin's father was a lighthouse keeper and his mother was a mermaid from the undersea land of Atlantis. As Orin grew up, he learned that he could live on land and underwater. He decided to use his powers to keep the seven seas safe as Aquaman.

CREATORS

SHOLLY FISCH WRITER

Bitten by a radioactive typewriter, Sholly Fisch has spent the wee hours writing books, comics, TV scripts, and online material for more than 25 years. His comic book credits include more than 200 stories and features about characters such as Batman, Superman, Bugs Bunny, Daffy Duck, and Ben 10. Currently, he writes stories for Action Comics every month, plus stories for Looney Tunes and Scooby-Doo. By day, Sholly is a mild-mannered developmental psychologist who helps to create educational TV shows, web sites, and other media for kids.

STEWART McKENNY ARTIST

Stewart McKenny is a comic artist living and working in Australia. He has worked on dozens of projects for the world's top comic book publishers, including Dark Horse, Marvel, and DC Comics. His credits include DC Super Friends, Star Wars: Clone Wars Adventures, and Captain America.

J. BONE COVER ARTIST

J.Bone is a Toronto based illustrator and comic book artist. Besides DC Super Friends, he has worked on comic books such as Spiderman: Tangled Web, Mr. Gum, Gotham Girls, and Madman Adventures. He is also the co-creator of the Alison Dare comic book series.

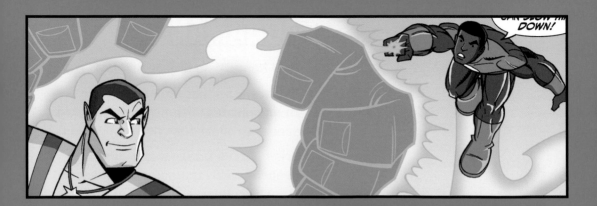

GLOSSARY

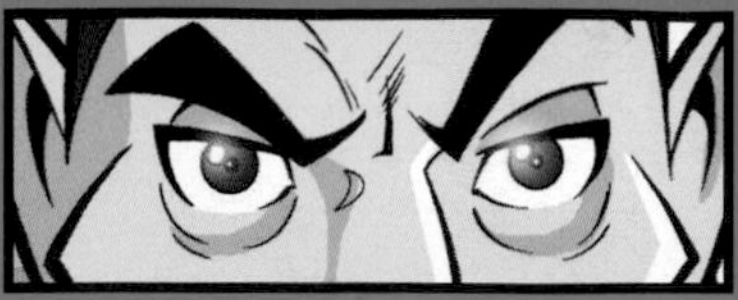

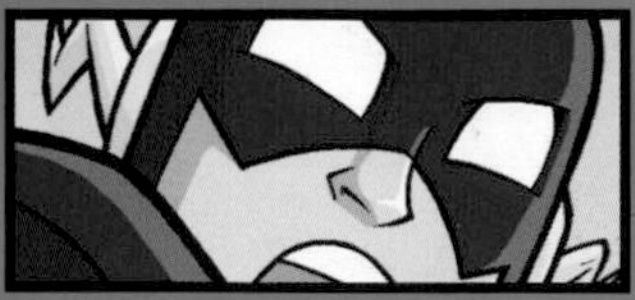

challenge [CHAL·uhnj]-something difficult that requires extra work or effort to do

confusion [kuhn·FYOO·zhuhn]-a lack of clearness or understanding

cowardly [KOU·urd·lee]-without courage

defenseless [di·FENSS·less]-without protection

distraction [diss·TRAKT:shuhn]-something that weakens your focus on what you are doing

emerald [EM·ur·uhld]-a bright green color

interplanetary [in·tur·PLAN·uh·ter·ee]-between planets

obviously [OB·vee·uhss·lee]-easily seen or understood

publicity stunt [puh·BLISS·uh·tee STUHNT]-an event or action that is carried out to get the public's attention

terrifying [TER·uh·fye·ing]-greatly frightening or scary

universe [YOO·nuh·vurss]-the Earth, the planets, the stars, and all things that exist in space

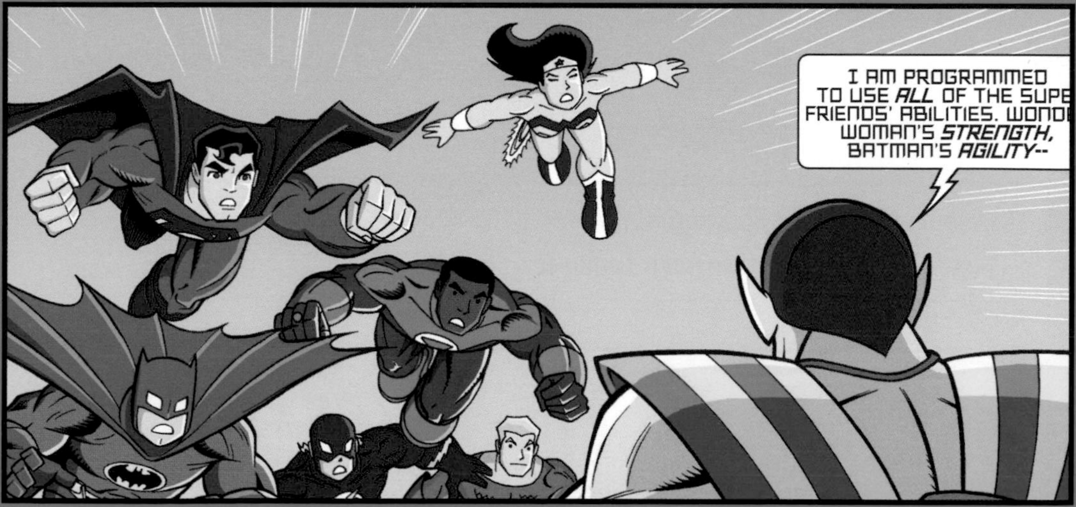
I AM PROGRAMMED TO USE ALL OF THE SUPE FRIENDS' ABILITIES. WONDE WOMAN'S STRENGTH, BATMAN'S AGILITY--

VISUAL QUESTIONS & PROMPTS

1. What day is it in this panel? How do you know?

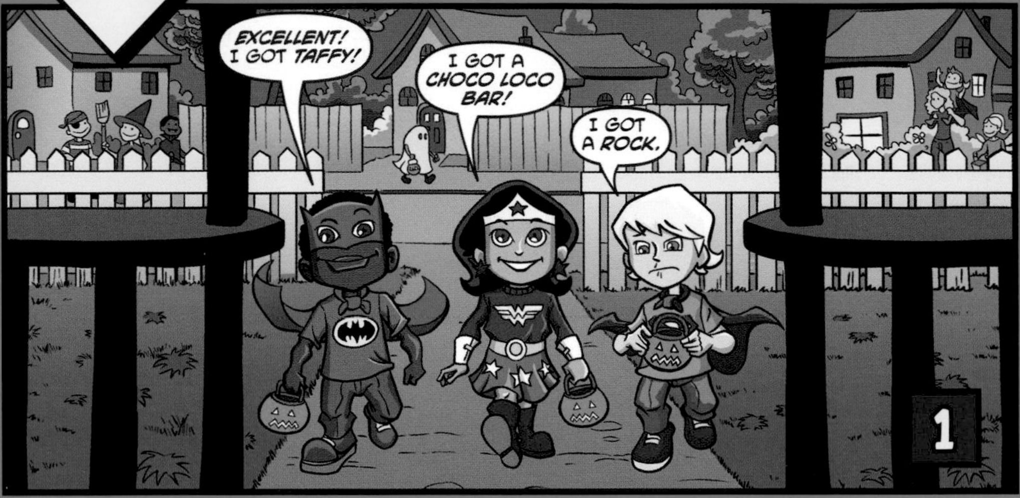
EXCELLENT! I GOT TAFFY!
I GOT A CHOCO LOCO BAR!
I GOT A ROCK.
1

2. Why is the Green Lantern forming a refrigerator with his ring? Read the banners on the stage for a hint.

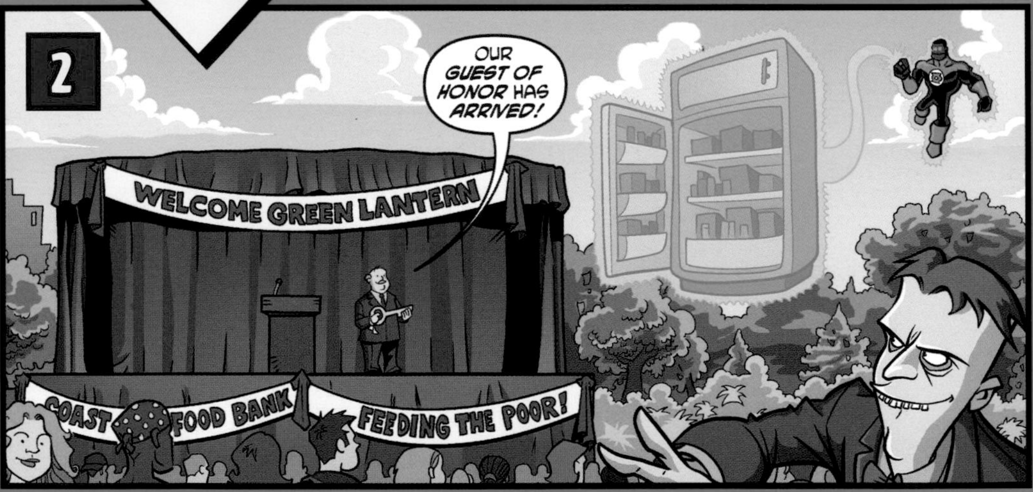
2
OUR GUEST OF HONOR HAS ARRIVED!
WELCOME GREEN LANTERN
COAST FOOD BANK
FEEDING THE POOR!

3. Explain what is happening in this panel. How is Green Lantern feeling?

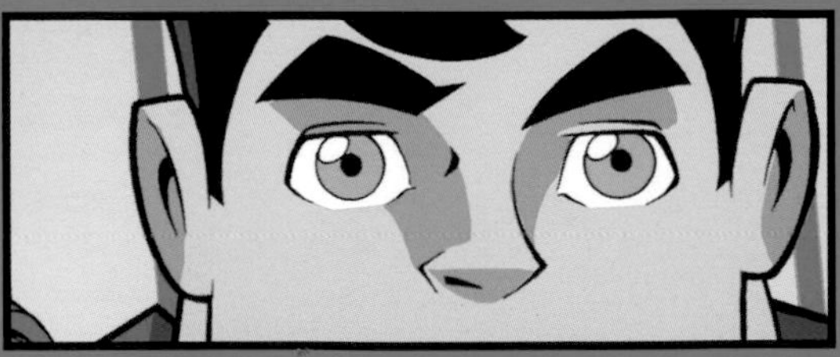

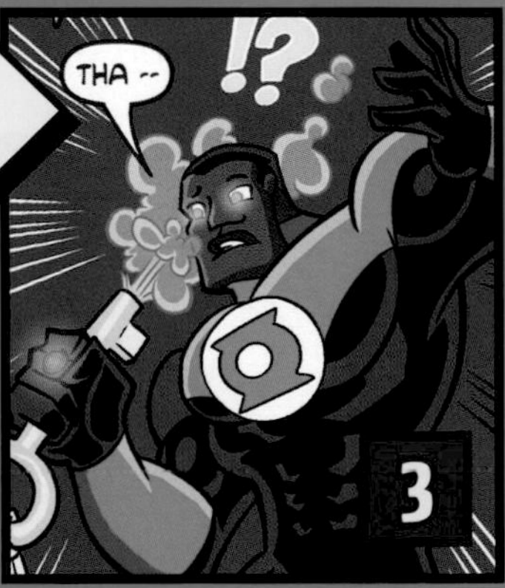
THA --
!?
3

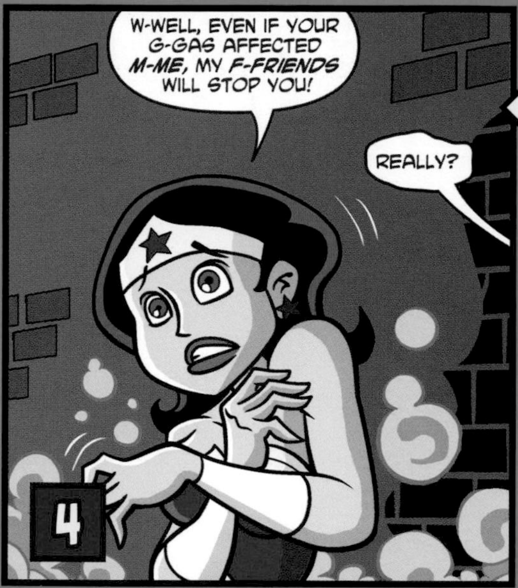
W-WELL, EVEN IF YOUR G-GAS AFFECTED *M-ME,* MY *F-FRIENDS* WILL STOP YOU!
REALLY?

4. What are some signs that Wonder Woman is scared?

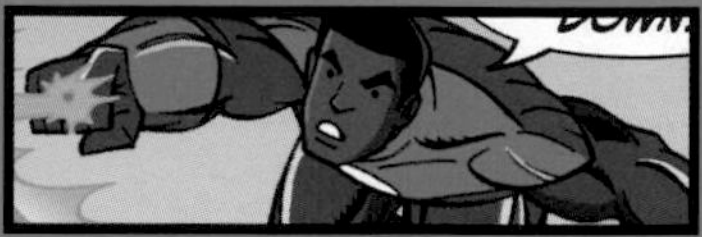

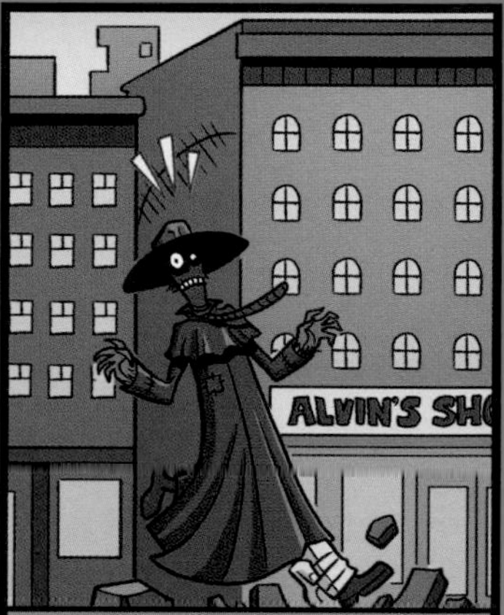
ALVIN'S SH

5. Explain what is happening in this panel.

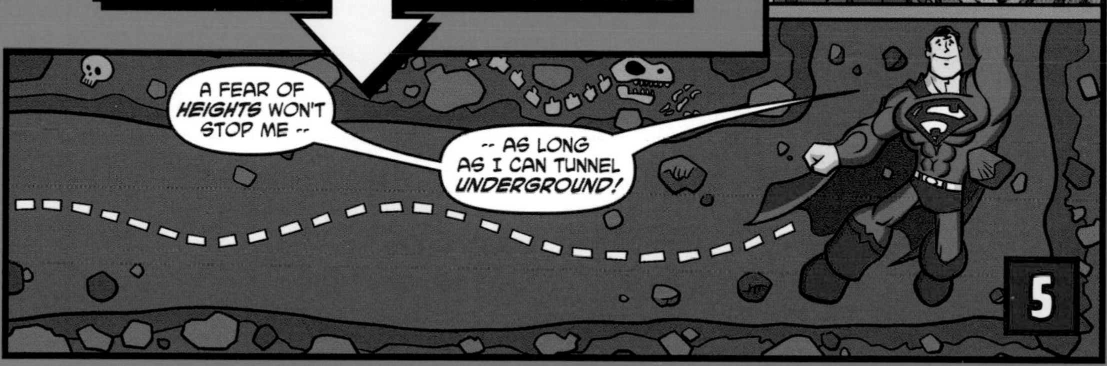
A FEAR OF *HEIGHTS* WON'T STOP ME --
-- AS LONG AS I CAN TUNNEL *UNDERGROUND!*

6. What does the yellow dotted line below show?

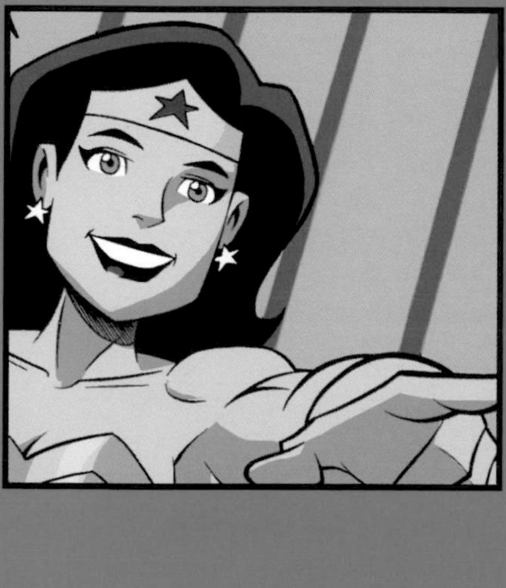

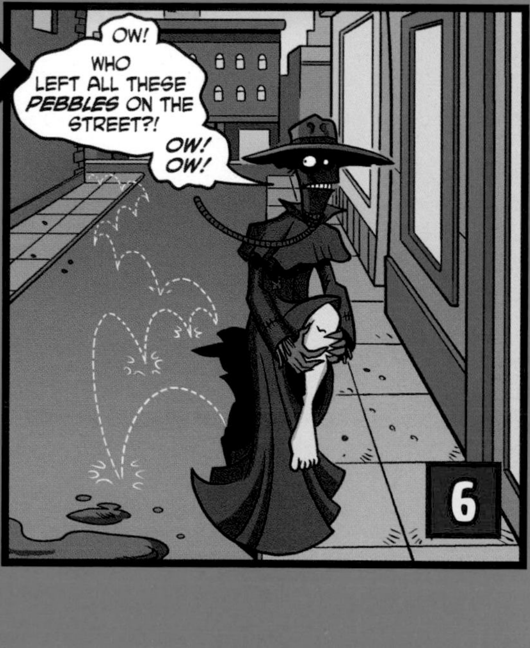
OW!
WHO LEFT ALL THESE *PEBBLES* ON THE STREET?!
OW! OW!

READ THEM ALL!

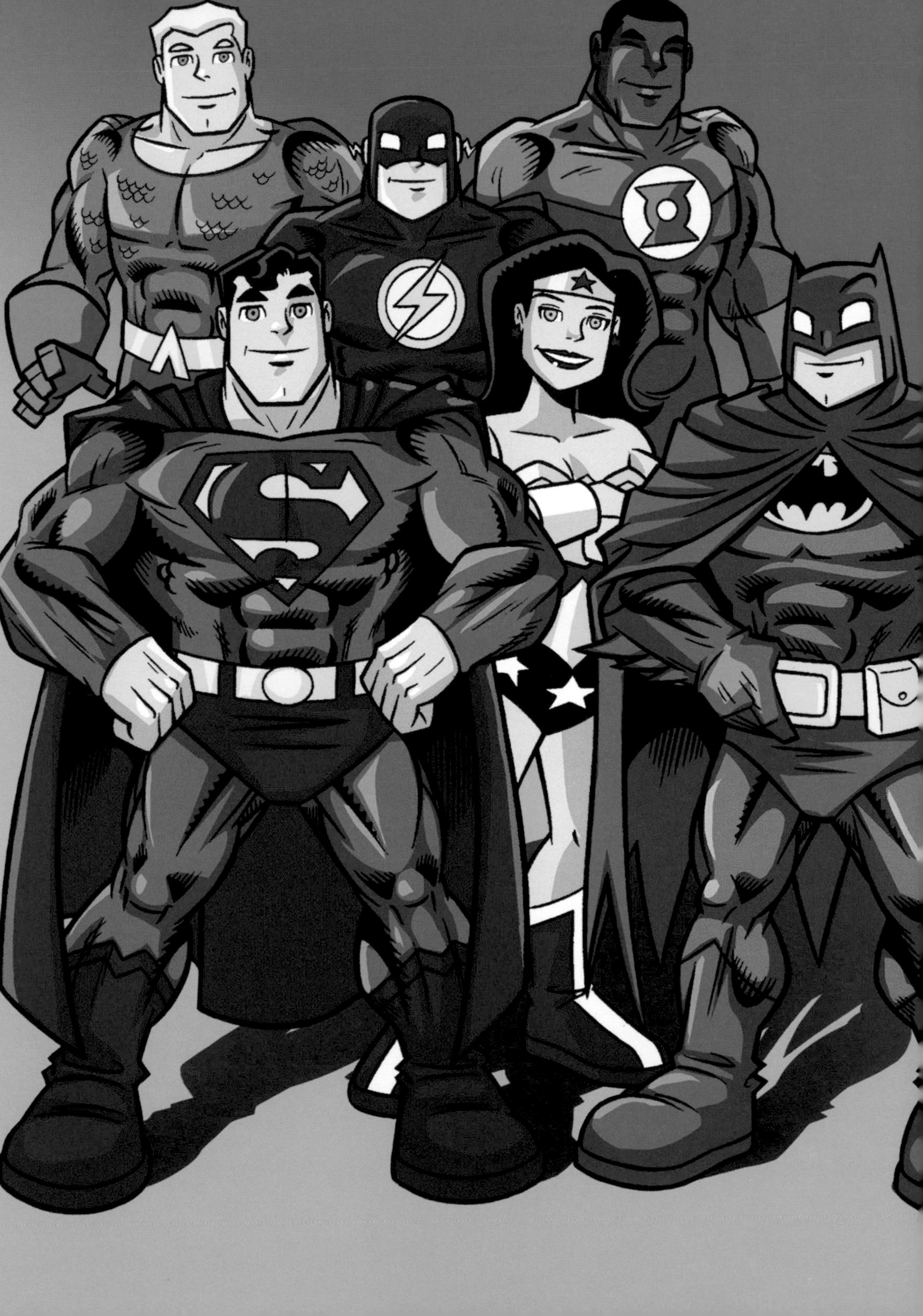

DC SUPER FRIENDS™

DC COMICS
DC SUPER FRIENDS
HUNGRY FOR POWER
Fisch · Brizuela

DC COMICS
DC SUPER FRIENDS
DINOSAUR ROUND-UP
Fisch · Ottolini · Staton

DC COMICS
DC SUPER FRIENDS
MONKEY BUSINESS

DC COMICS
DC SUPER FRIENDS
CHALLENGE OF THE SUPER FRIENDS
Fisch · Brizuela

DC COMICS
DC SUPER FRIENDS
APRIL FOOLS
Fisch · Brizuela

DC COMICS
DC SUPER FRIENDS
WANTED: THE SUPER FRIENDS
Fisch · McKenny · Moy

DC COMICS
DC SUPER FRIENDS
JUST MY LUCK
Fisch · Brizuela

DC COMICS
DC SUPER FRIENDS
NOTHING TO FEAR

ONLY FROM...

STONE ARCH BOOKS™

a capstone imprint www.capstonepub.com

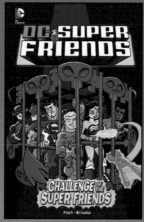